I Look Like You

I LOOK LIKE YOU

A NOVEL

BROWER

Printed in the United States of America.

Designed by Annie Fuhrman.

ISBN-13: 978-1542641661
ISBN-10: 1542641667

I Look Like You

1

On the platform outside Kansas City's Union Station, as he waited to board the train, Andy felt shaky and weak. His ankles were tight, his back was sore. He felt like shit, really. He should've at least gotten some sleep, but when he got home a few minutes after 5:00 a.m. from his job as the night manager at the Stoddard Hotel in downtown Kansas City—a luxury hotel with headquarters in Chicago— he had instead spent the two-and-a-half hours before the 7:37 a.m. departure packing his suitcase, jogging forty-five minutes on the treadmill at his apartment's gym, and reading his parents' obituary for probably the tenth time.

They had died at the same time. The newspaper had printed a joint obituary.

There were a few dozen people also waiting, Andy somewhere in the middle of them, yawning and limply clutching a large coffee from the kiosk inside Union Station. As always, the coffee was giving him hints of a kick (more like a nudge), while leaving his stomach feeling murky and unhappy. He should've at least eaten breakfast rather than just that single serving of flaxseed crackers he had consumed before hustling out the door. The crackers had been somewhat good but had left his stomach still empty, and his mouth dry and chalky, like how it had mornings after smoking a cigarette, during that phase years ago when he had tried to look and act like James Dean.

"Okay. Who's next?"

Andy looked up to see an Amtrak attendant waving him over.

He handed his ticket to the attendant who skimmed it. Andy considered removing his sunglasses—was that rude or pretentious to just leave them on like this? But he kept them on. He looked better with them on. He was also wearing scuffed brown shoes and a light gray jacket that mixed well with his dark blue (practically black) jeans. His hair had recently been cut by his stylist of choice, Elise, and he had it slightly slicked back with the grooming clay the salon sold. He was thirty years old, five-foot-six, and had been skinny most of his life, the kind of malnourished-looking, never-gaining-weight-despite-eating-fast-food-multiple-times-a-week skinny that annoyed his more plump family members and friends, much to Andy's delight—people were jealous of *him!* But the last year or two, despite mostly cutting out fast food and instead eating more like an adult should, the weight had weirdly started to pile on, five pounds here, five pounds there, putting him at a good twenty pounds heavier than a couple years ago, the reason for which still unclear. Age? A change in metabolism? He still wasn't technically obese, and he knew telling people he was concerned about his increasing waistline would only elicit responses like "you've gotta be kidding me" and "oh my God, you're ridiculous," so he kept these thoughts to himself.

"Okay." The attendant scribbled a seat number on a small piece of blue paper and handed it to Andy.

Andy's stomach growled again in rebellion, his body still unhappy with just the pathetic handful of flaxseed crackers and watered-down coffee this morning. Or maybe the coffee was too acidic. Or maybe he actually was allergic to gluten or dairy despite the tests he got at the doctor's saying otherwise. His stomach was always making noises, seemingly always upset about something. It had been for years. "You just got yourself a rumbly tummy," his doctor had said once, flicking Andy's gut with an index finger.

He stepped onto the train, carrying his lone suitcase and backpack. That was enough for this weekend trip to Chicago. He had a couple outfits, his laptop, the always-growing collection of power cords for various electronics (the number of white Apple cords alone made Andy feel like he had signed a blood pact with the company), and of course a black suit for Saturday.

He wedged his suitcase in the rack along with the others on the first level of the train, and then climbed to the second level to look for seat C24.

He had always liked Amtrak fine. It was easier than driving, the seats were roomy, and most importantly, it wasn't a plane—planes being one of his phobias, along with snakes and riding on a motorcycle. The trip from Kansas City to Chicago took a little over seven hours, giving him plenty of time to sleep and to complete the only item on his to-do list for today: writing a speech for Saturday.

Andy found C24, an aisle seat, next to a man who looked near seventy. The man was leaning on the windowsill, gazing outside. His hair was thin but still hanging in there.

He turned to Andy. "Oh, hi," he said, smiling. He had on a blue striped button-down shirt, the kind of simple shirt they sold at mall department stores.

Andy started to place his backpack in the overhead compartment but then opted to put it at his feet.

"Hi," Andy said. He removed his glasses. He wondered if his eyes looked bloodshot. They felt that way.

He took a deep breath, and put his sunglasses in the mesh netting on the back of the seat in front of him. He had only been standing for maybe four minutes, but sitting down felt amazing.

"So where you heading?" the man said. "I'm Jerry by the way."

"Andy." They shook hands. "Chicago."

"Chicago! Beautiful city. Windy, isn't it?"

"Yep. That's the reputation."

"I wonder how many times I've been there." Jerry looked up, appearing nostalgic. "A lot. By my age if you haven't been a lot of places, you know, what are you doing with your life?" He shook his hands as if he were ringing someone's neck. "Heh-heh. I'm just kidding. So what brings you to Chicago?"

"Um." Andy considered giving a fake answer—why open the flood gates?—but instead he opened the flood gates that were his mouth and said, "I'm from there, but this particular trip is for a funeral. My parents'."

"Your *parents*? Oh. Oh. I'm so sorry. Oh boy." Jerry stared down, looking at his clasped hands, his thumbs rubbing each other, as if trying to erase something. "Man, your parents were probably around my age? Crud." He shook his head. He swallowed. "Well, I figure, if you make it to sixty, you're lucky. You've won already. You know?"

Andy squinted in confusion. His parents had both made it to sixty, yes, but no further. That didn't seem like much of a win.

"Still very sad," Jerry said. "Hey, let me know if I can do anything."

Everyone, it seemed, had offered to "do anything," whatever that meant.

"Do you have any other family?" Jerry said.

Andy sipped at the coffee. He wouldn't be getting to sleep anytime soon.

"Just a twin brother. Taylor. That's who I'm staying with."

"*Twins*. Oh wow. You guys must be close. Something about in the womb, right? Gestating together? That's got to be an amazing connection. Well, at least you still have that."

"Mmm-hmm," Andy said, not bothering to correct Jerry on his assumption that twins = close. He and Taylor hadn't even talked since the accident. It had been Taylor's wife, Candice, who had told him the news.

He had just returned from the gym (he had done crunches so frantically a girl had told him to "chill out or you're gonna crack a rib") and was preparing a dinner of kale, mixed vegetables, and asparagus, missing the days in his early twenties when he had consumed hot dogs, fries, and Coke for dinner without any shame, when she called.

"Oh, I'm so sorry, Andy," Candice had said in a choked whisper.

". . . Sorry about what? . . . Is everything okay? What, does Taylor want to borrow money again?" He had laughed, he later realized, too loudly.

"Your parents . . . they're . . . Andy, they're dead."

". . . What? What do you mean?"

She then explained in a rush of words: his parents had been driving home from a late dinner in Chicago, and his father had apparently fallen asleep at the wheel, slamming the car into a streetlamp, killing them instantly.

"At least it was instant," Candice had said.

Instant.

Was instant the way to go?

"Taylor's too upset, so that's why I'm the one to call," Candice had said. "Oh, is there anything I can do?"

"No, no . . . oh . . . wow . . . um . . . no, it's okay. Thanks. We'll, well, we'll talk soon. . . . Yeah. . . . Okay . . . bye."

On the train, a voice came over the intercom. "Hello, passengers! We are looking at a time of 7:40.

We're about to leave beautiful Kansas City on this crisp April morning, with service all the way to Chicago, with stops along the way. As always, thanks for choosing Amtrak. As a reminder, there is no smoking. . . ."

When the intercom shut off, Jerry said, "I only lost my parents about ten years ago, actually. Though, not at the same time. I can't imagine what that must be like. Just *poof*, gone like that."

"Yeah, it was . . . it's been hard." It had been, but in some ways Andy was more upset by how *not* upset he was. There had been no crying, no pounding fists on the wall, no cursing God. Mostly just quiet.

He hadn't seen his parents since Christmas, the last time he had visited Chicago. Since then they had talked sporadically, last talking a month or two ago. Taylor was the one closer to them. Taylor needed to be in some ways, as they had still been giving him money, despite him being married, not to mention thirty years old, while Andy had vowed since college to never ask his parents for a cent if he could help it.

The train lurched forward and began building in speed as it eased out of the station.

"Goodbye, Kansas City," Jerry said to no one in particular and then pulled out a bag of peanuts, shaking a few into his upturned hand.

"Here, want some?" Jerry said, holding the bag to Andy.

"No, that's okay. Thanks." Andy took a pull on his coffee, which was still kind of disgusting, but for $1.25 it was okay. He could afford better coffee, for sure, but he was thrifty with money—or cheap. One of those. And come to think of it, now he would probably save around two-hundred dollars a year from not having to buy his parents birthday or holiday presents anymore, not to mention the inheritance that would be coming his way. So at least there was—*I'm an asshole, a real* fucking *asshole*, Andy thought, sinking further into his chair. Where did thoughts like that come from? And why had he had so many of them the last few days? These *pluses to losing your parents* thoughts.

The stressful week and lack of sleep had messed with his head.

The sun was spiking through the windows, so Andy put his sunglasses back on as he fidgeted in his chair to get comfortable. It was time to get some sleep, and maybe that was possible now that Jerry had perhaps stopped talking.

"Oh!" Jerry said. "Is the sun bothering you?" He grabbed the curtain and pulled it closed.

"No, it's okay. Really."

"Nah, I don't mind. Not good for my eyes either. Smart move bringing your sunglasses."

Andy pulled off the sunglasses and held them out to Jerry, perhaps feeling like he needed to do a good deed. "If you'd like to wear them, you—"

"Oh no, nonsense." Jerry held up his hands in protest. "But thank you."

Andy put the glasses back on and then rustled in his backpack, finally extracting his iPod and headphones. He felt bad, but headphones were a nice way of saying, "I can't really talk now."

"Ooo," Jerry said. "I got one of those a year or two ago. Pretty nice, but I find myself still listening to CDs. Call me old-fashioned." He chuckled.

Andy put on his headphones.

"What are you listening to?" Jerry said.

Andy had been listening to some Neko Case, Future Islands, and Nick Drake lately, but what was the point of telling this guy? He wouldn't have heard of any of them.

Andy shrugged. "Not sure. Still trying to decide."

"Well, I'll let you get to it."

Andy nodded, switched to the Nick Drake, and turned the volume up and up, letting the sound surround him as he closed his eyes, feeling bad that he was hoping the man would please just stop talking.

When he opened his eyes, he noticed, to his relief, that the seat next to him was empty. He looked at his watch. 10:15. About two hours of sleep, but he felt even worse. A headache was beginning to form, jabbing at his forehead, and his stomach's upset rumbling had only grown in intensity.

"Oh, you're awake," Jerry said from behind, as he walked up the aisle, carrying a cup of coffee with the Amtrak logo on it.

Andy pulled in his stiff legs, so Jerry could squeeze past and land in his seat.

"I got you some breakfast earlier; hope you don't mind."

Jerry dug into his tote bag and handed a small box of Corn Flakes to Andy.

"Oh. Thanks," Andy said, sitting up.

"Those will clean you out all right," Jerry said, laughing. "Sure do to me."

Andy peered at the side of the box and was dismayed to see it contained high fructose corn syrup and more sugar than he'd like in a cereal, but rather than be rude, he opened the box and poured some into his hand before sliding the flakes into his mouth. His stomach shuddered in retaliation. He would have to pop some antacids later.

"So a twin, huh?" Jerry said, as if picking up from an earlier conversation. "I have a brother. Well . . . technically, *had* a brother. Not a twin though. He died in Vietnam."

"Really? Jeez, I'm sorry."

"He was younger, which made it harder to bear. My kid brother, y'know?" Jerry funneled more peanuts into his hand. "But whether you agree with the politics or not, you must have respect for our armed forces. An extreme sacrifice."

"Of course."

"Well." Jerry placed the empty peanut bag at his feet. "Do you and your brother look alike?"

"Yeah. Almost exactly. Though he's a little bigger." But then Andy realized, with his recent weight gain, maybe they were closer in size than he had thought, an idea that bothered him. Being better than his brother in finances, career prospects, and health had always been a badge of honor.

Their parents had done the classic twin things: dressing them alike, making them share a bedroom until well into high school when Andy and Taylor finally insisted they get their own rooms, even though that meant Andy had to sleep in the poorly-ventilated basement. His parents, like a lot of other parents of twins, had treated them as a "unit" in a sense, rather than as individuals; his parents had enjoyed the novelty of twinship. Andy and Taylor's classmates had too, frequently urging them to switch classes to pull a prank on the unsuspecting teacher. *Come on, it'll be so funny!*

Andy slid some more cereal into his mouth. Honestly, he hated being a twin. Taylor did too. To everyone else, they were something to gawk at. *You two are identical! I'm seeing double! Ha!* It was weird having a literal doppelganger, a 3-D mirror, someone to always be compared to.

Jerry brushed his hands together, flicking away the stray peanut crumbs, and then sipped his coffee. "Ah," he said in satisfaction. He scratched at his scalp. "Well, you full? I got some more peanuts." He produced another bag from his tote bag.

"No, I'm good. Thanks for the breakfast."

"Sure thing." Jerry reached into his pocket and pulled out a roll of Tums. He held them out to Andy.

"Oh, thanks," Andy said, grabbing two.

"Stomachs are made for being upset. Lord knows I know that."

Andy grinned. Well, they had one thing in common.

After another ten minutes of small talk, Andy, realizing he wouldn't fall asleep again anytime soon or get anything done here, grabbed his backpack and rose to his feet, his knees popping loudly.

"Well, I'll see you later," he said.

"Oh? Okay," Jerry said, looking disappointed. He turned to stare out the window, shuddering against the cool temperature inside the train.

Andy walked down the aisle, passing an Amish family who appeared to be using cell phones. Eventually he reached the observation car a couple cars down, where a few people were sitting, talking in small groups or staring at phones, tablets, or books.

He pulled out his laptop and set it on his knees. He opened a Word document and saved it as "Eulogy.docx." Candice had asked him to speak for a few minutes at the funeral. Taylor would speak too.

After hovering his fingers over the keys for what felt like a minute, he typed *Death can happen in the snap of a finger*.

He recoiled. *Death can happen in the snap of a finger*? While not necessarily false, it sounded way overly poetic and pretentious. He held down the "delete" key, wiping out the text.

Okay, he told himself, just write something, and I can edit it later.

He typed *My parents were great people. I like you am saddened by their sudden passing.*

Passing . . . why was it that people could never just say *died*? They had to say someone passed away, like it was some "woops!" moment, even if in this case it was. Still, they had crashed into a streetlamp. His dad had fallen asleep. If he was so tired, he shouldn't have driven in the first place. Andy's mom was perfectly capable of driving a car and had thousands of times. It wouldn't have violated some husband/wife law of the universe to let the wife drive for once.

Andy took a deep breath, willing himself to chill out, to not be so cold and angry. *Jeez*, shouldn't he have at least cried by now? Shouldn't he have felt like his life was irrevocably changed? Was this what baby boomers meant when they said younger generations these days were too self-absorbed? Too obsessed with their online personas?

Andy peered up, watching the fields of grass pass by the window.

"Give it back!" a boy shouted.

Andy looked over to see two brothers, probably six or eight, fighting over an iPhone.

"Share. Brenton! Share," the boys' mom said, in between texting on her own phone. She didn't look much older than Andy.

Andy turned back to his laptop and tapped on the keys, hoping this rhythm would drum an idea into his head. He had never been much of a writer or public speaker—that was more Taylor's thing—but he wanted to come up with something good. There were no second takes at funerals. And maybe he was feeling like he had been a shit of a son—just getting them gift cards for their birthdays and holidays, rarely calling, just kind of keeping to himself rather than telling them about his life and what was going on—and this was one way to make it up to them.

Walter and Helen Canton were devoted parents, members of their community, employees, and family members. They worked hard and loved harder.

He stared at what he had just written. It all sounded phony, like "Eulogy Speechwriting 101." Members of their community? Sure, they had volunteered a couple times, but what did that really mean? They had hated a lot of things about Chicago; his dad had ranted constantly about the homeless people, his mom about the freezing winters. What could Andy say that wasn't totally trite? And "loved harder"? That sounded almost pornographic.

Andy turned his attention back to the window and the passing fields zooming by the train—or rather, the train zooming by the passing fields. They still had several hours until Chicago. There wouldn't be much to look at on the way.

He glanced down at his laptop but nothing came to mind.

He wished he had a pen or pencil, so he could chew on the non-writing end while in thought, but instead he just had the lingering taste of Corn Flakes in his mouth.

"That's it!" the mother nearby said, startling Andy.

She snatched the iPhone out of her son's hand.

"Mom! That's not fair!"

"Yeah! It was my turn! Mine!" the other boy said.

"No, it wasn't! No, it wasn't!"

The mother, without a word, put the phone in her purse and then returned to texting on her phone.

Andy and Taylor had fought constantly as kids.

The younger boy began crying.

"Moooom," he said. "I'll be good. Pleeeease let me have it back." He bowed his head in her lap.

"Go talk to Dad," the mother said, glancing up from her phone, which was inches from the boy's head.

The younger kid ran away to the adjoining train car.

"Here ya go," the mother said, reaching into her purse and handing the iPhone to the older boy who flashed a conspiratorial smile.

Andy reached into his own bag and found some Tylenols he quickly popped in his mouth, before he remembered he hadn't packed any water. He was out of coffee too, so he tried to build up saliva in his mouth, and when that didn't work, he finally just bit down, crushing the tablets into a tangy dust that he swallowed, wincing.

He looked back at his computer, the cursor blinking as if to say, "You're not done yet."

Maybe the problem was his lack of knowledge about his parents, outside of the surface details: they were Walter and Helen Canton. They married in 1975. His mother had had at least one miscarriage before having Taylor and Andy in 1983. Her maiden name was Wyatt. She and Walter had met at college, where he studied economics and she French.

Maybe there was a French saying he could throw in the speech, something that sounded deep and relevant. But what? His mother had rarely spoken French around the house. After graduation she had worked as a secretary for a car dealership—speaking only English, Andy assumed—before becoming a mother and ditching a day job altogether. His dad, meanwhile, had worked his entire career at a company that did *something* with money; Andy still didn't understand what. Mostly just trying to create more of it. He had brought Helen and the kids to a few company outings, awkward picnics with heaps of clammy potato salad, or baseball games (always the Cubs and never the White Sox, for some reason), where he and Taylor were told to be on their best behavior, and if so, they would get McDonald's for dinner.

His parents had been relatively good parents. They had seemed relatively happy in their marriage and their lives from what Andy could tell.

Relatively.

Relatively.

They had been neither remarkable nor boring. Neither rich nor poor. They had done okay for themselves. They had played by the rules. With politics, they had been moderate, voting for Reagan twice, but later Dukakis and Clinton, and then later George W. Bush. In religion, they had chosen to believe.

Andy wiped the sleep out of his eyes. He still felt in a daze, so maybe he wasn't totally emotionless about his parents' deaths if you counted "in a daze" as an emotion. Taylor had always been the more emotional one.

When the Stoddard Hotel told Andy they were opening a Kansas City location and wanted him to be the night manager, he had said yes almost immediately, despite having next to no knowledge of Kansas City. Was it just country music? Backwards politics? Failing sports teams? A crumbling city?

Still, he welcomed the challenge, while Taylor would probably never leave Chicago, and in some ways, might never fully get his shit together, as he was now on his third graduate program in a third subject (none of them completed so far), this time International Leadership, as if he had a future brokering NATO treaties. His current job was an unpaid internship at an agency in Chicago that did, what, Andy didn't know, other than not pay their interns. Luckily the money from their parents and his wife's salary as a lawyer at a small firm downtown had helped them rent at least a decent apartment in Lincoln Park.

Andy returned his fingers to his laptop.

My parents were devoted to us and each other. They were inseparable.

He once again stopped. Was that true? Yeah, his parents had spent a lot of time together, but was it just out of marital duty, rather than a yearning to be with each other?

He dug around in his backpack for a book someone had loaned him at work. Maybe he needed a break from the speech. He just wasn't inspired yet. The book was called *The New Thirty: How to Turn the Dreams of Your Twenties into Realities in Your Thirties!* It was written by a guy named Baron Ritter. Andy turned over the book. Predictably, the author in the photo looked to be early forties, slightly graying, wearing an expensive suit, and smiling with his arms folded in a look of "Don't you wish you were me?" success. From the bio, he sounded like a junior Tony Robbins, one of those intense "self-actualization" guys probably exhausting to be around.

Andy had casually mentioned to a coworker on Tuesday that he was interested in self-improvement. He had always worked hard and tried to be disciplined, but this renewed interest had most likely cropped up in the aftermath of his parents' death, when his own mortality became apparent, so it was time to get with it now or risk not achieving . . . whatever it was he wanted to achieve. He was happy working in the hotel industry. He took hospitality seriously. He had done well at the Stoddard since starting fresh out of college at the Chicago location. Eight years of loyalty; eight years of listening to nightly customer complaints; eight years of co-workers who sometimes failed drug tests (and were promptly fired); eight years of never enough towels in a guest's bathroom. Still, he liked it. The Kansas City location was thriving in the revitalized downtown Power & Light District, and he liked to think he was part of its success. He didn't love working nights—it made having a regular social life difficult, and the last time he had been on a date or even gotten laid had been . . . six months? Eight?—and nighttime was when the most intense things happened: guests fighting, drunken misadventures in the hotel hallways, people breaking into the closed pool, hotel staff members fucking in a storage closet among the stacks of towels and toilet paper—but Andy didn't mind the challenge.

Andy opened the book and turned to the prologue.

When I turned thirty, I looked in the mirror and thought, "I'm not all I could be." I was working at a hedge fund, pulling down 150K a year, and I still wasn't happy! Can you believe that!?

Andy shut the book. He already hated this guy.

The crying boy came back into the observation car.

"Mom! Mom! Dad says I should get it. Jefferson had it yesterday."

The mother glanced up from her phone.

"Yeah, okay. Whatever."

She grabbed it from the older son and handed it to the other kid.

"What! That's not fair!" the one apparently named Jefferson said.

The mother shrugged.

Andy shoved his laptop and the piece-of-shit book that he'd have to tell his coworker he "wanted to read but just don't have the time right now" into his backpack and stood up, sending a wave of dizziness through his head. Spots blinked in front of his eyes. Ugh. He needed some sleep.

He steadied himself, grabbing a nearby chair. He looked at his watch. It was a little after 11:00. Might as well go down to the snack car and get lunch. Maybe a heavy lunch could sedate him for an afternoon nap.

Down in the snack car, he surveyed his options. There was nothing remotely healthy except some browning bananas and apples that looked equally decayed, so he sighed and chose the personal pizza option, which the attendant microwaved for him.

"This is some good stuff," the attendant said. "I like it myself."

The pizza was no doubt loaded with preservatives, processed cheese, and other no-nos, but in some ways, Andy felt, maybe he could ease up on his diet for a few days. He had wanted to eat healthy on this trip, but it was hard to eat well while traveling. Or at least that was a convenient excuse.

Still, he already felt the pangs of regret, and he had yet to put any food in his mouth.

The microwave dinged.

"All right," the attendant said. He grabbed it. "Ooo! Ooo! Sucker's hot."

He placed it down on the counter, shaking his fingers.

"You think I'd know by now," he said, chuckling.

Andy also bought a Starbucks Frappuccino—mocha flavored—even though he knew it was basically five-percent coffee and ninety-five percent sugar. Sugar—another thing he needed to cut out entirely. Everywhere he looked there were things he needed to stop eating or drinking. How did people make it through their days, their lives, and not succumb to all the crap easily at your disposal everywhere?

He looked around the car for a place to consume his shame meal but every table was spoken for, so he headed back to his seat, hoping Jerry would be gone. But when he returned, he saw Jerry not only sitting and gesturing animatedly with his hands, but also a woman, around fifty, heavily made-up and with an abundance of jewelry, sitting in Andy's seat.

"It's a disgrace, is what it is," Jerry said, before seeing Andy. "Oh sorry, bud."

"It's okay. I can find a seat somewhere—"

"No, no," Jerry said.

"Sorry, hon," the woman said.

"Andy, this is Diane."

"Hi," Diane said, beaming.

"You never know who you'll meet on this train," Jerry said. "My lucky day."

"Are you . . . famous?" Andy said.

"No," she giggled. "Hardly. Only to my friends! I was just walking by, and this character over here starts talking to me."

"Ah." Andy spied a large wedding ring on her left hand. Was her husband here somewhere? Had Jerry not noticed the ring?

"Well," Jerry said, "maybe we should go to the observation car."

"Good idea," Diane said, standing up. "I could use a change of location on this stuffy train."

Jerry soon followed.

Andy sat down in his vacated chair, excited to be alone.

"Well, you are joining us, aren't you?" Jerry said. "There's plenty of room."

"Oh, I was just gonna eat lunch." Andy pointed down in embarrassment at the pathetic cheese pizza—more like a pile of cheese on a supposed piece of bread—and his Starbucks Frappuccino, which, save for the coffee, looked like a drink for children.

"Nonsense. Plenty of room. Come on. You can eat your food there."

Andy relented and followed them to the observation car.

Luckily, the mother and her fighting sons were gone.

Jerry found a table and took a seat, while Diane grabbed the seat on the opposite side of the table. After a brief deliberation, Andy sat next to Jerry, placing his food and coffee on the table and his backpack by his feet.

"Mmm," Jerry said, "that pizza smells good. Too bad I can't have any, or I'd get one of those myself." He looked up at Diane. "The doc's got me on Lipitor and other things to quote-unquote 'address the health concerns of a man my age.'"

"Yep, I'm barking down that door too—but for women, of course."

"I've been trying to exercise more like the doc said. Well, then of course my joints go to crap, and now I'm taking chondroitin and—blah, Andy, just enjoy it while you can."

"Yeah, I've been trying to cut out this kind of food too," Andy said.

"What? Nonsense. Enjoy it while you can."

"For real, hon," Diane said.

Andy took a bite of the pizza, which was still incredibly hot. He quickly doused the fire with the

Frappuccino. Why he was consuming more caffeine when he wanted to fall asleep, he didn't know.

"And my hearing's getting bad too," Jerry said, throwing up his arms before slapping them on the table. "I figure I'll just spontaneously combust one of these days." He pulled some Tums out of his pocket and popped them in his mouth.

"My pinky. . . ." Diane stuck up her left pinky. "Anytime it's gonna rain, it starts tingling. This kind of *bzzz-bzzz* feeling." She clasped her hands. "Well. So, you're father and son, I take it?"

"Oh no," Jerry said, chuckling. "Andy's just a nice guy I met on the train."

"Oh that's sweet," Diane said. "What brings you on the train, Andy? I like hearing why people are on the train."

"My parents died, and I'm going to their funeral."

"Oh. Oh dear, I'm so sorry."

Andy swallowed another bite of pizza.

"And here we are talking about our own silly problems," Diane said. "I'm sincerely sorry." She reached forward and touched Andy's hand.

"No, that's okay," Andy said. "Sorry, I'm a little sleep-deprived, so I'm a little punchy. I didn't mean to be rude."

She gave Andy's hand a friendly squeeze and then let go.

"Apparently, Diane's going up to Chicago too," Jerry said. "She makes her own jewelry, and there's a big convention this weekend."

Diane held up her hands in a "ta-dah!," showcasing the multiple rings and other pieces on her hands and wrists. "Started out as a passion project, but when I lost my job, well, I took it full-time."

"See, that's great," Jerry said. "I could use a passion project like that." He nodded to himself. "Well, if you're ever looking for a partner, I might just be interested."

"Oh, that's so sweet of you." She turned to Andy. "You know, women always like jewelry as a gift. I have a lot of my products on board if you'd like to take a look. Seriously, it's no problem. I can go get some right now."

Andy swallowed another bite of the pizza. "That's okay. I'm single."

"Well, a little jewelry could change that." She winked before growing serious. "Oh, you're not gay, are you? Sorry. If you are, that's totally fine. I have a gay nephew. I unfortunately don't have any jewelry for men."

"No, I just said I'm single. Being single doesn't mean I'm gay."

"Sorry. Ha. I'm just trying to be P.C.—there's always something new. Well." She unclasped her purse and pulled out a card. "Let me give you one of my cards at least." She handed it to Andy.

Diamonds by Diane: When you want to Sparkle!

"Thanks," he said. "Well, I think I'll go back to the seat and get some sleep. Thanks for the card."

"Sure thing, sweetie," Diane said. "And I'm really sorry about your parents."

"I'll see you later, bud," Jerry said. "Get some sleep. You look exhausted." He clapped Andy on the back.

Whether it was the Frappuccino or how his mouth was still on fire from the pizza, he didn't feel particularly tired. Still, when he got back to his seat, he stashed his backpack at his feet, folded his arms, and closed his eyes. He sat there for five or ten minutes, but sleep predictably didn't come, so finally he opened his eyes and pulled out his laptop again to work on the funeral speech. He began typing, *My parent's death is a reminder of how short life can be. Life is fragile. Take the opportunities you have and go with them. Like my parents did.*

Ugh. He stopped himself. He sounded like a televangelist. He was supposed to say some nice words, not give a sermon.

Maybe he needed to brainstorm more. He opened a new Word document, saved it as "Eulogy Ideas.docx," and started a list:

Mom liked football, Dad liked baseball. Maybe something about that?

Dad played the bass guitar in a band in high school. His favorite band was the Animals, he's the only person I've ever hear say that.

Mom used to watch Seinfeld and laugh so loud, the neighbors would call to make sure everything was ok. <- Ok, use that. That's funny. Maybe??

We went to Cedar Point for 3 family vacations. One time we heard people in the hotel room next to us having sex and mom laughed and laughed. Ok yeah that's good. She liked to laugh a lot. Laughing is good. Dad laughed some, too. But probably a normal level of laughing. Maybe shouldn't mention sex in a church though??

*Dad taught both Taylor and I how to drive at the same time. He once said "When I'm old and blind, you'll be driving me around". That might be good to say, except they died in a car accident. Dad was never blind but he fell asleep at the wheel so he was blind in a way.

Andy stopped himself. This was getting depressing. Well, maybe that was a sign he was on the right track. It was a eulogy after all, and it would be nice to feel *something* but still. . . .

He put his laptop away. He still had a couple days before the funeral. Maybe Taylor could help him come up with something, or maybe Andy would insist just Taylor talk. Did it really matter if Andy said something too? Either way, he and Taylor would probably fight over it.

He sat back in his chair and out of the corner of his eye saw Jerry walking his way, alone. Andy immediately closed his eyes and mimed being asleep.

He heard Jerry scoot in front of him and sit down in the window seat, breathing audibly.

Andy was continuing to play sleep, when he heard Jerry whisper, "It's okay. I saw you were awake. I get it. Sorry to be a bother."

Andy winced but didn't know how to respond, so he kept his eyes closed, waiting for this moment to pass. Still, he could recognize, he *was* a real asshole.

It had been a weird, weird week. Or had he always been an asshole like this?

When the train pulled into Union Station in Chicago, a few minutes after 3:00, Andy grabbed his backpack and stood up.

"Oh, don't forget these," Jerry said, grabbing Andy's sunglasses from the mesh net hanging off the seat in front of them.

"Oh, thanks." Andy looked down at Jerry still sitting in his seat. "Aren't you getting off too?"

"Nope."

"Don't you have to? It's the end of the line, isn't it?"

"I've actually just been riding the train across the country back and forth for a few months now."

". . . Really?"

"Yeah."

"Can I ask why?"

Jerry shrugged. "Gives me something to do. Gives me a sense of purpose in my 'old age.' I've needed that."

"Ah. I had no idea."

"You never asked," Jerry said, shrugging again.

"What about Diane?"

"Oh, her? It was just nice to talk to someone. Even for just a few minutes." Jerry gazed into the distance, looking wistful. He gave a weak smile, far removed from his earlier bouncy body language. He turned his head to peer out the window, which now just showed the inside of the train terminal, a poorly-lit cavernous structure that resembled a factory at night.

Andy stared a second longer at Jerry, feeling like apologizing for something, but he didn't know what to say, so he joined the herd of people leaving the train, all pushing to get off quickly, all pushing to just get off the train.

2

Andy exited Chicago's Union Station, passing a
couple homeless men calling out to people for
change, and walked into downtown, the Thursday
afternoon streets teeming with people and cars,
movement and sound. He still loved Chicago. He
wasn't sure why he had left it so easily three years
ago. It was a place of activity, a beating pulse, while
Kansas City, at times, felt like stalled rush-hour
traffic and "see, things are improving . . . aren't
they?" newspaper articles.

But maybe everyone has to leave home at some
point.

The weather was low fifties—pretty nice—and
predictably slightly windy, tussling his previously
slicked-back hair and dangling his bangs over his
forehead, causing him to frequently reach up, trying
to get everything back in place. Next, he pulled up
the zipper on his gray jacket but stopped at about
chest level, as that seemed to look good on him.

He had his backpack over his shoulders, and he
was pulling his suitcase, which bounced on the
occasionally uneven sidewalk. He resented the idea
that he might look like a tourist, some out-of-town

guy walking around with an "aw shucks" vibe at the "big city," so he made sure to walk quickly, eyes focused straight ahead, to not give off any sense of being lost or unfamiliar with the terrain.

Last night, when things had gotten quiet at work, and he had been sitting in the back office, he had taken off his shoes and, slightly unprofessionally, put his black-socked feet up on the desk, his suit coat tossed on the other chair in the office, as if it were a person he was interviewing for a job, and he had wondered what it'd be like to return to his hometown for the first time as a person with no parents. Maybe it was overly serious books or overly serious movies that had ingrained in him the idea that this would be a profound moment, that he would in fact now feel like a lost out-of-towner in his own hometown, but as he stood at the southwest corner of Jackson and Canal, people in business casual or construction uniforms standing by him waiting for the crosswalk lights to change, he felt nothing. He was just . . . *here*. It just so happened that his parents weren't anymore.

After riding the Brown Line train to the Fullerton stop, he began the three or four block walk to his brother's apartment.

The cramped conditions on the train had made him hot, the after-burn still going even though he was now on the street, so he grabbed his jacket zipper and descended it another couple inches or so. He knew he was preoccupied with his looks—not that he thought he was good looking, but that looking good was important to him and was a desire he was forever chasing. This was perhaps more a concern of the unattractive or "average," as if small decisions like zipper height or positioning of hair could save you from being cast into the "not particularly good looking" category, a category Andy thought he unfortunately always had one foot in, or at least if he didn't really try, might find both feet planted there. This concern was yet another difference between he and Taylor, who frequently wore oversized t-shirts or ruffled sweaters that just had the Nike logo or the name of some college he had never attended but had bought at a gift shop in the college's town. This maybe would've been more understandable if the clothes said Harvard or Cornell—the kind of place that elicited "Harvard, huh? Wow!" type reactions—but two of his sweaters said University of Miami and Mercer, hardly conversation starters, especially for someone who had never attended there or knew anyone who did.

Taylor's apartment was in a three-story brick building off a street that Andy saw had undergone some changes since he had last been there: a new Mexican restaurant, a couple more bars, a new thrift store. The front door of the building was unlocked, so he stepped over the welcome mat, which had a mostly-faded "l" making it instead declare "we come," and walked to his brother's ground-floor apartment, apartment number two.

He was about to knock when he saw a picture of his parents taped on the door. His first thought was, "Oh, come on. . . ." Taping pictures to your front door seemed like something you did in college (before a person on your floor inevitably drew dicks on the photo), but then he took a closer look. The photo looked recent, maybe within the last year? His parents were sitting outside somewhere, both dressed up. His dad's hair had been noticeably thinning over the last few years, while his mother had let hers go gray after years of dyeing it. Still, they looked good. They looked happy. They looked content.

The front door opened.

"Oh, Andy," Candice said.

He had yet to knock or audibly signal he was waiting by the door.

She grabbed him in a hug.

"I'm so sorry," she said, sounding like she was tearing up.

Andy placed his hands on her back, trying to return the squeeze she had given.

"Thanks," he said.

Candice separated from him, still holding him at arm's length.

"You're doing okay?"

"Yeah, I'm not too bad," Andy said.

She shook her head and pulled him in for another hug.

"Really," Andy said. "I'm okay."

Candice had always been maternal, the type to feel everyone's pain a little bit, to hold eye contact when you asked her a question, to remind you to grab sunscreen if it was sunny outside. Taylor was lucky to have her. They had met in college, dating their senior year and getting married soon after. It was surprising they hadn't had kids yet, as Candice grew up in a large family—four or five brothers, two or three sisters (Andy had lost track)—and seemed to love people, but maybe they were just waiting for Taylor to finish school. In the meantime, when she wasn't working, she volunteered—a few hours a week at a pet rescue place and as a Big Sister in the Big Brothers Big Sisters program. Maybe a few other things too.

She was one of those people with seemingly boundless energy, or stamina maybe, someone who made everyone else appear at least somewhat lazy.

Taylor was lucky to have her.

Candice finally let go of Andy. "I feel so bad for you guys."

"Yeah, it's tough. But thanks." They shared a solemn smile. "So . . . where's Taylor?"

The look on her face turned slightly cold but then returned to her maternal demeanor. "He's inside. Sorry, come on in."

After he passed the coat closet, opting to keep his jacket on, he walked into the living room, which opened into the kitchen, all one large room. The portion of the room designated as the living room was decorated modestly with just a couple pieces of furniture, two ferns, a thirty- or thirty-two-inch flat screen TV, and white IKEA shelves stocked with DVDs, CDs, and even a CD player, the same one Andy had gotten when he turned twelve, and had finally thrown out five years ago when the notion of owning an actual CD player anymore seemed horribly dated and unnecessary. The couch in front of the TV had a couple fraying pillows and several books, including one titled *International Leadership Ethics: Volume 6.* A few pieces of art hung on the wall, probably things Candice had acquired. No way Taylor had compiled them, with his indifference to interior decorating, not to mention his lack of contributing any sort of money to their household other than what he had poached off his parents. His contributions had probably been limited to the CD player and a few DVDs, as well as a Ryne Sandberg autographed poster near the TV, which looked rather out of place.

The apartment was by no means a shit-hole, but its overall shabbiness made Andy feel further sorry for Candice. She could likely do better than this but was probably pulled down by Taylor's student loan debt and his "toss it anywhere" mindset.

As if reading his mind, Candice said, "Sorry, it's a little messy. Taylor and I have been very busy. My Little Sister had a choir concert last night, and . . . well, all that's happened."

Taylor looked up from the kitchen table, where he was typing something on his laptop, and then rose to his feet, stepping over tentatively.

"Hello Andrew." Cordial yet distant.

"Hey Taylor." Andy nodded.

Here would be a time to hug, but they remained a few feet apart. They rarely touched. It had just always felt weird, the two of them sharing any sort of physical intimacy, as if the nine months in the womb had been more than enough.

Taylor adjusted his glasses, but they remained crooked. He was, predictably, wearing a boxy sweatshirt, this one with a Champion logo.

"Thanks for coming," he said.

"Yeah . . . well. . . ."

It suddenly felt warm in the apartment, so Andy completely lowered and detached the zipper on his jacket but kept the jacket on, despite still feeling hot.

"Oh cool," Candice said. "I love your jacket. Members Only. Nice."

"Thanks."

Taylor smirked. "Are you in an eighties phase now? Not James Dean anymore?"

"No."

Hoping to change the subject, Andy turned to the back bedroom, squatted down, and held out his arms.

"And where's Duffy? Come on, Duffy," he called out to Taylor and Candice's dog, a terrier whose small frame and white fur made him disappear in the Chicago snow. As far as Andy could remember, Duffy had been one of the first "we're in this for the long haul" acquisitions Taylor and Candice had made before later getting engaged and then married.

But Andy remained squatting, not hearing the patter of dog feet on wooden floors or the jingling of Duffy's collar, and instead only hearing Candice and Taylor's feet moving slightly, the floor creaking.

"Are you being serious?" Taylor finally said.

Andy looked over his shoulder at his brother. He got to his feet and faced him.

"We had to put Duffy to sleep a month ago," Taylor said. Candice placed her hand on his arm. "I posted all about it on Facebook."

God, Andy was a dick, it was again becoming clear. He had, one night, annoyed at Taylor for something, unfollowed his brother's posts. They no longer appeared in his feed.

"Sorry," Andy said. "I must've missed it. I didn't know. My bad. I'm . . . so sorry."

"That is unbelievable," Taylor said. "Seriously, I—" He paused to inhale and exhale deeply, the whole thing seeming to calm him down. "It's . . . it's been a bad few days. I haven't been taking it particularly well. Our parents are *gone*."

Andy slowly nodded. "It's weird. I don't think it's hit me."

"Really? It has me, for sure."

Candice ran her hands over Taylor's back.

"It's okay, Andy," she said. "You're just grieving in your own way. Everyone grieves differently."

"Yeah . . . that might be it."

"Did you see what we put up?" Taylor said, pointing to a large family photo by the living-room window. It had to be from the early nineties, when Andy and Taylor were eleven or twelve, with gaps in their smiles where braces hadn't yet corrected, both of them with awkward nineties bowl cuts, their parents looking equally bland in their pastel clothes, their dad sporting a mustache—something he had tried for just a couple years before calling it a "silly mistake" and shaving it off—and their mom still wearing her hair very long, something she had only given up the last ten years or so, trimming it to a bob.

Andy didn't have any photos of his parents—at least physical prints. He probably had some on his computer somewhere, but he couldn't remember.

Taylor moved closer to the photo. "I know it's pretty old, but I thought it'd be nice to have up." He stared at the photo, looking like he might get choked up. He lowered his head and then turned to his brother. "Well." He pointed to a green box on the recliner, with a couple blankets and a pillow by it. "We got out the inflated mattress. We just need to fill it up. We have a pump somewhere." He looked to his wife. "Do we have some extra towels too?"

"Yeah, of course," Candice said.

"Thanks," Andy said. "That's really nice of you guys."

"No problem. I'm glad you chose to stay with us," Candice said.

Andy had planned on getting a hotel room—specifically the Stoddard, where he could stay for free—but Candice had insisted, practically begged, he stay with them, something he really didn't want to do out of preserving some sort of family peace, but he had given in.

But then again, Taylor hadn't acted too unbearable . . . so far. Still, family was like alcohol sometimes: in small doses, it could be fun, fine, add a kick to something, but more than that, and you woke up sick, your hand clutching your forehead, vowing to "not do *that* again."

But this weekend, he'd try to make it work the best he could.

For dinner, Candice selected an Italian restaurant, the name of which Andy couldn't pronounce. Inside they were greeted by a hostess, beautiful, maybe twenty-three at the most—old enough—and she led them to a table, in a sense acting like a guide as the restaurant was dark to the point you almost needed a flashlight to navigate it, and the employees, likewise, wore all black, making them look like floating heads bobbing around the room.

After they took their seats, the hostess flashed a grin and walked away, Andy watching after her, her tight black skirt and black high heels, her curvy hips jostling *left to right, left to right*, as she moved back to the hostess stand.

"Yeah, like you have a chance," Taylor said.

Andy turned back to the table.

"How *are* the ladies?" Candice said, giggling.

"Not really any," Andy said, looking at the menu.

The last girl he had quote-unquote hooked up with had been someone actually staying at the hotel last fall, and while that had felt fun and edgy—*hooking up with someone at my place of employment!*—he had still made sure he was off work during the actual consummation of the hook-up—that moment when front desk flirting became hotel room sex—and had then left out a side door to avoid any puzzled looks from his co-workers as to why he was leaving the hotel at 8:00 a.m., a few hours after his shift had ended, his eyes tired, his hair and clothes in disarray.

Candice said, "We should set Andy up with—"

"He's here for a funeral," Taylor said. "We have a lot of stuff to do anyway."

Candice grimaced and then looked back at her menu.

"Ugh, I'm starved," Taylor said. He motioned to a waiter who rushed over.

"Yes, sir?"

"We're ready to order."

"Oh, well, Brandon's your server."

"Okay. So, where is he?"

"I'm sorry, sir. He'll be over shortly. He's helping another table."

"Oh. Okay. Well, we are ready."

"Yes. Sorry for the delay, sir."

The server hurried off, disappearing into the darkness.

"Don't be rude," Candice whispered.

"We've been here a couple minutes and haven't had contact with anyone other than the hostess. Andy knows hospitality; that's just bad. He didn't even take our drink order. He could've at least done that."

"Still."

"Servers bitch if you don't leave a huge tip," Taylor continued, "and then take a photo of the receipt and post it on Facebook in an effort to ridicule you when the low tip might've been their fault. I'm just saying."

"Well," Andy said, thinking it over. "Yeah, that is kind of bad, but you don't need to. . . ."—*family peace*—"well, yeah, I don't know."

He reached for his water, taking a deep sip.

Eventually, Brandon—whose nametag said "Joseph"—came over, apologizing profusely, with a basket of complimentary bread, and took their drink orders, writing none of it down, perhaps trying to do the razzle-dazzle of waiting tables: memorizing orders.

When he left, Taylor grabbed the biggest piece of bread and then passed the basket around.

"How much longer do you have in your program?" Andy asked, reaching for a slice of butter, before he stopped himself. Butter would no doubt improve the bread—what *hadn't* butter improved?—but it was pure fat. The large piece of bread sitting on his plate looked equally like a haven of carbs and regret, but he would look dumb putting it back, and . . . well. . . .

With his mouth still full, Taylor spoke up. "It keeps me very busy, but . . . after this semester ends, a year or so. Though I might go for my Ph.D., which would mean another four or five years on top of that."

Andy swallowed the first bite of bread and then set it down. "Your *Ph.D.*? In International Leadership? There's value in that?"

"My advisor strongly recommended it."

"Of course he did."

"He's a woman."

"Okay, sorry—*she*. But of course she did. It's in the university's best interests to keep their students in programs until the very possible end, especially ones who do well, which I'm guessing you are." Andy had done well in school, but Taylor had always done better. Taylor was a smart guy. Just not always in the subject of common sense.

"Mostly As. A journal publication too."

"Yeah, so of course they want you to stay. More for them than for you. College is a business like anything else at the end of the day. But sooner or later you got to . . . you know, get a job. I mean, it's not like you're in med school here."

Brandon/Joseph returned and dropped off their drinks.

When he left, saying he'd back in just a moment to take their orders, Taylor spoke up, staring at his glass of wine as he addressed his brother. "I'm not sure you know what you're talking about."

Andy opened his mouth to speak but stopped. Maybe he was just thinking back to that period when he had considered applying for a graduate program in Anthropology or just *something*, because college had been enjoyable—learning was enjoyable—during that time when the thought of spending the rest of his life in a hotel that had a room labeled "soiled linens" seemed unbearable, but luckily time had helped him get over this nostalgia for college life, and he was now happy with what he did for a living, and it didn't cause him to stay in school until his mid-thirties, only to graduate with mountains of student loans, and be only able to get low-paying employment, which according to what he read in newspapers, seemed to be the fate of many people who pursued Ph.D.s.

"There's a real market for doctorates in the field right now," Taylor said.

Andy took a sip from his wine—white wine; he should've gotten red. "And you need a Ph.D. to do . . . whatever it is you plan on doing? You'd actually move away from Chicago?"

"Well . . . no, but there are several companies in Chicago who work with companies and governments all over the world. Someone with my skills could be very valuable."

"And you're really that into international relations? I just never knew you were so into it."

"I am. I think it's important. You don't have to understand it, but it's important to me. Dad had a master's degree, and mom would've, but then she had us. I feel like I owe it to them to do something worthwhile and important."

And what does your wife think about this?, Andy wanted to ask but kept his mouth shut. Chances are "what does your wife think" hadn't occurred to Taylor, nor would carry much weight.

The waiter popped out from the dark.

"Okay, are we ready to order?" he said. "So—okay, I'm guessing you get this all the time, so sorry in advance, but you two wouldn't happen to be twins, would you?"

"What gave it away?" Taylor said, glancing up from his menu.

"Well—I—"

"Yeah, we're ready," Andy said. "We'll let the non-twin, Candice, take 'er away. Candice?"

While they waited for their food, Taylor pulled out his phone. "I mapped out a plan for tomorrow. How about we get started cleaning Mom and Dad's house at 7:00 a.m.?"

"*7:00 a.m.*"

"Yes, 7:00 a.m."

"Can we make it 8:00?"

"No."

"8:00 will be fine," Candice said.

Taylor looked to Candice.

"Okay, 8:00 is fine," he said.

Taylor continued from there, outlining his plan for the day, including how long they should allot for a lunch break, and at what time, as well as estimated travel time to and from their parents' house. He sounded more like a foreman than Andy's brother.

"Is there really so much stuff to do?" Andy asked. "I was kind of hoping to see some old friends." Though, he didn't exactly know whom he was referring to.

"Yes, there's a ton. This weekend should be about family anyway. You're here for a funeral."

The waiter returned to the table with their meals.

"Okay," the waiter said. "We have the Penne Pasta over here." He placed the plate in front of Candice. "Careful, it's hot."

"Are you even sad about what happened?" Taylor whispered to Andy.

"And we have the—oh." The waiter stopped, seeing their faces. "Is this a bad—"

"No, we're fine," Andy said, motioning for him to continue.

Once the waiter had dropped off the last item and grabbed the rickety metal stand that held up the tray, snatching it up with a loud *ping*, he rushed away from their table.

"Well, are you?" Taylor said.

"Of course I am."

"Well, you don't show it."

Andy grabbed his silverware, shaking his head. He had no response.

"People show their emotions in all different ways," Candice said. "At Big Brothers Big Sisters, we learn that people—"

"Yeah, I know. People grieve differently." Taylor's face softened. "You . . . I mean, you said that earlier."

Candice stared straight ahead and then grabbed her wine glass, slowly holding it up. "Well." She cleared her throat. "For Mr. and Mrs. Canton."

Andy and Taylor exchanged glances, before raising their own glasses and joining Candice's in the air.

"For Mom and Dad," Taylor said.

". . . For Mom and Dad," Andy said.

3

When they returned to Taylor and Candice's place, it was barely past 8:00. Andy scanned his mind for the names of Chicago friends—maybe he should give some a text or a call, try to get a group together, do something. What else was he going to do tonight?

Taylor sat down on the couch. Candice chose a separate chair.

Andy stood there, fingering his phone in his pocket, debating on what to do.

"Take a seat," Taylor said. "I have something to show you."

Andy plopped down on the couch—he'd call his friends in a bit—picking a spot a couple feet from his brother. He felt bloated, full, like he had been repeatedly punched in the gut by a large Italian man. He kept clearing his throat, as if something were lodged there. He shouldn't have had that second glass of wine, or cleaned his plate at dinner. But really, maybe it was the restaurant's fault. Despite not being an Olive Garden, the portions were similarly gargantuan, as if a dare: "Go ahead and try to eat all this." It was Italian food, served with an American philosophy, and Andy was the patron who had forgotten the option of eating a modest amount—one that wouldn't cause him to wake up repeatedly in the middle of the night to dash to the bathroom to empty his overtaxed bowels—and taking the rest to-go.

Yeah, maybe it'd be a good idea to just sit for a while and digest.

Taylor grabbed three remotes, hitting a few buttons on each. The TV and nearby DVD player whirred to life, blue lights flicking on.

"I've been going through old family videos I had converted to DVDs a couple years ago," Taylor said. "And I made kind of a medley of some of the best stuff."

"Okay." Andy cleared his throat. "I thought you were so busy with school work."

Taylor continued pressing buttons.

"They're really pretty cool," Candice said.

The first video started, the footage grainy and choppy with occasional lines of static shimmying up and down the screen. It took Andy a minute to figure out what was happening: several kids running around a kitchen, parents hovering over them, the women with poofy eighties hair, the men with hairy legs and shorts practically as short as daisy dukes, as if they were ready should a basketball game break out. A cake was in the center of a kids table.

"Our fifth birthday," Taylor said.

"Oh yeah, we got those fire engines, right?" Andy said. Soon after that birthday, he and Taylor had become infatuated with firefighting, playing in the backyard with a hose, dousing out imaginary fires, wearing tall black boots and snow pants wherever they went, as if they were firemen ready for action. But like anything, a year later they were on to something else. Mailmen. Dentists. Baseball players.

In the video, Taylor and Andy were both wearing the same corduroy pants and striped shirts. Same haircuts and party hats—red—while the other boys and girls wore assorted colors. Even now, Andy felt annoyed—had his parents just been too lazy to buy them separate outfits? Why had they insisted on dressing their kids so stereotypically *twin*? Buying them the same gifts.

"Watch this," Taylor said, smirking.

Five-year-old Andy blew out the candles before Taylor could, sending the smoke into Taylor's face, who coughed and teared up, jumping up and down as if trying to escape a wasp attack, eliciting laughter and sympathy from the adults. Their mom came into the frame, hugging Taylor and wiping the tears and smoke out of his face. She too had large, hairspray-enveloped hair, her body thin, her skin tan. Five-year-old Andy, meanwhile, seemed oblivious to what had happened, instead looking between the cake and one of his friends who was reaching out to grab some frosting, before Andy pushed his arm back.

Jeez, he was a jerk back then too?

Had he meant to blow smoke in his brother's face?

Taylor and Candice laughed as the video transitioned to their second grade Halloween costumes—both cowboys. Andy laughed a bit too but mostly felt uncomfortable. Was this how they were going to spend their night? Two or three hours of this?

"Unfortunately, Dad's in almost none of these," Taylor said. "He was always filming. The plight of the person behind the camera, I guess."

"You guys were so cute," Candice said, looking touched at both the boys holding up pillowcases of their candy haul for the night.

"*Were?*" Taylor said, smirking and raising an eyebrow.

"You know what I mean," Candice said, laughing.

Jeez, Andy thought, there was a time they could fill a bag with candy and eat it in a frenzy without a second thought. Snickers, Reese's, Twix. Even gross candy like Almond Joy. Didn't matter. They would eat it with reckless abandon, because they were kids and they could. In some ways, Andy didn't know what the point of these videos was, or nostalgia in general. To remember you were once younger, in better shape, happier, more care-free, still had parents' who were alive? If anything, the clip made him hate to see what trick-or-treating looked like now. Parents having to inspect all the candy for razorblades or only accepting healthy "treats" like protein bars or organic bananas. Asking for gluten-free candy or something with antioxidants rather than food coloring and chemical names they couldn't pronounce. Insisting the candy be made locally and with only natural ingredients. And the thing was, if

Andy were a parent, he'd probably be insisting on these things too.

The video continued from there, the clock on the wall of Taylor's apartment pushing past 9:00, with no apparent end in sight, clips of Christmas mornings, Boy Scout ceremonies, family camping trips, random moments such as Andy singing the Beatles' "I Want to Hold Your Hand" at an elementary school talent show, horribly off-key, and with a cheesy Beatles wig that even now embarrassed him—for some reason his parents had let him go solo on that one, Taylor nowhere in sight. In all the videos, the twins getting older and taller, while their parents seemed to turn grayer and get heavier near their waistlines, more slumped over, more jowly.

Taylor had clearly put some time into this. Not only looking through hours and hours of footage and selecting clips, but stringing them together, inserting transitions, adding some music in spots. Andy wondered, why wasn't Taylor doing this for a living? He clearly had a talent for it, but Andy knew better than to mention it. The last thing Taylor needed was another new career idea or possible graduate program to consider.

"I can't believe they're gone," Taylor said.

"They were such good parents," Candice said.

"I know," Andy said, though mostly he just wanted the videos to stop. He had just never been one to take photos or videos, to document things like this.

"I talked to mom last week," Taylor said, still looking sad as he turned to Andy. "She was saying how much she wishes you'd call more."

Andy slumped further in the couch. Why was his brother telling him this now? It wasn't news—he knew his parents had always wished he'd be a part of their lives more—but still . . . why, right now?

"So how many more videos are we going to watch?" Andy said.

Taylor paused the DVD. "I thought you'd enjoy this."

"No, you did a really good job. Seriously." Andy attempted to sit up, though he still felt sluggish and a little dizzy and sleep-deprived. "But . . . it's just . . . you guys want to get a drink somewhere? You know, get out for a bit? Might be good to—"

"We have beer here," Taylor said.

"Yeah, you want one?" Candice said, immediately jumping to her feet.

"Thanks, but I was thinking, you know, let's go somewhere."

"What? Why?" Taylor said.

"Just one drink," Andy said. "I'll pay. Seriously."

Candice grinned. "Oh that's so sweet. Sure. I could go for one."

"No," Taylor said. "We have a lot to do tomorrow. We should get our sleep. Besides, didn't you have two glasses of wine at dinner? You should be sated."

Sated. His brother used words like *sated.*

"Whatever," Andy said, rising to his feet, the blood rushing to his head, causing him to wobble like a bobble-head doll.

"Oh hey—are you okay?" Candice said, stepping toward him.

"I'm fine." He caught himself on the back of the couch and steadied his feet.

"You're fucking drunk," Taylor said.

"No—I've just been sitting for a while. I just—I haven't been feeling great all day."

"Well then you should stay home and get some sleep," Taylor said.

"Do you want some Ibuprofen or something else?" Candice said. "I think we have—"

"No, that's okay. Thanks though. I'm—I'm going to go out for a bit. I'm not staying home all night and watching . . . y'know, the *E! True Hollywood Story* about our family." Andy winced at his pathetic joke. "Candice, you want to go?"

Candice pursed her lips and then looked at Taylor, before turning back to Andy. "I guess I'll just stay home. Sorry."

"Yeah . . . okay. That's okay."

Andy walked over to the dining room table and grabbed his keys—why, he didn't know, as none of his keys would do anything in Chicago—and shoved them in his pocket.

"*One* drink. We have stuff to do tomorrow," Taylor said, more and more sounding like a parent. By all appearances, he and Candice were fitting nicely into traditional gender roles—the caring, nurturing mother, while Taylor was the pissed-off disciplinarian.

Andy put his gray jacket back on, zipping it up halfway.

51

"Yeah, I know," Andy said. "Stop saying that. Sure you don't want to come, Candice?"

She shook her head. "No, I better not. Have a good time though."

"I will."

Andy stepped outside the apartment building into the small courtyard out front. It was noticeably chillier than earlier. He zipped up his jacket, almost to the top, even though it looked better with the zipper at half-mast. Still, he was cold, shaking slightly. He hadn't even packed a heavier jacket for this trip. *Fuck*, he was an idiot. It was Chicago, a place he had lived twenty-seven years, and he had forgotten how brutally cold it could get here even in April.

He saw someone had left an empty pack of Marlboro cigarettes nearby, which he immediately stepped over to and kicked, the whole thing moving maybe three feet.

His brother was a controlling, whiny dick.

Andy considered himself a responsible human being, but Taylor . . . there was a difference between responsible and just fucking uptight. It was as if because Taylor was married, he thought he was the real adult, while Andy was some child who needed to be kept in line.

Andy pulled out his phone and scrolled through his contacts before he found some Chicago friends and began calling them, hoping some would be up for hanging out, grabbing a drink—or *two* if they felt like it.

". . . Hey! Great to hear from you! What's up? . . . Oh, I can't. Just finally got the kids to sleep. . . . Angelica's two now, can you believe it? Crazy."

". . . Sorry, man. Work in the morning. Ya know?"

". . . I'm in Toronto. This place is so awesome! You gotta visit. I'm out with some of my co-workers right now, actually. I better get back. Woo! Oh, Canada, baby!"

". . . Andy, I'm married now. I don't think my husband would go for it. . . . No, he doesn't want to come either."

". . . Dude, I heard about your parents. So sorry, man. . . . To*night*? Like, now? Sorry, can't. Yeah, no, I can't."

And finally, he reached the last Chicago contact in his phone.

". . . I've been sober three years," Zack said.

"Oh," Andy said. "That's great. Yeah, congrats, man." It was weird congratulating someone for no longer drinking, when you were hoping to be drinking in less than five minutes. And still, since when had Zack had a drinking problem? He had never seemed out of control or anything, though they had only hung out a few times—and well . . . maybe Andy didn't know his friends as well as he thought, or at least these people he had lost contact with over the last few years. "Well, we can do something else, like, well, there's probably a coffee shop open somewhere. It'd be great to catch up."

"Sorry," Zack said, "but I really don't like to do caffeine after 8:00 p.m."

"Well, they have decaffeinated probably and—"

"I'm sorry, but not tonight."

"Oh. Okay, then."

Andy placed his phone back in his pocket and considered his options. Maybe he should just return back inside, but no, that felt like admitting a defeat of some kind.

Out of the corner of his eye, he saw the empty Marlboro pack, taunting him, and without a second thought he ran up to it like a NFL kicker and booted it as far as he could, the pack this time flying onto the sidewalk twenty feet away.

"Hey, watch it," a man, walking his dog, said. "Jeez, man."

The dog sniffed at the pack before its owner briskly pulled him away.

"Oh. Sorry. Sorry."

Embarrassed, he remained standing there, with his hands shoved in the pockets of his jacket, shivering against the spring breeze.

4

Andy walked down the street and turned onto Adams, where he saw several bars, restaurants, and stores.

A neon sign in the window of a cell-phone repair place flashed "Get Your Fix!!"

He wandered for several minutes before, feeling like he just needed to choose *something,* he stepped into the Golden Cup, where he was immediately hit with jangly psychedelic rock coming from the overheard speakers. A coffee grinder similarly clattered with a hypnotic, slightly grating, rhythm. About half the tables were occupied, almost everyone staring at an Apple product of some kind. Headphones on most ears.

He walked to the counter. A tall, lanky barista looked up from his phone.

"Hey man, sup?" the barista said slowly.

Andy scanned the options on the large menu on the wall. Tea, no matter how caffeinated, always put him to sleep, and coffee would probably wreak further havoc on his over-taxed stomach, but he shrugged and said, "Just an iced coffee. Large."

While the coffee was being prepared, he skimmed the flyers and business cards on the nearby bulletin board. A self-defense class. A petition to have more leash-less dog parks in the city. A "rootsy improvisational" band named Funk Guzzle playing this weekend at Busted Acorn. "Soul Smash," a DJ spinning soul records at Double Drive, happening tonight. A seminar on polyphasic sleep next month at some place called The Sleep Temperance Society.

"Here ya go, bro," the barista said.

Armed with his coffee, Andy found a table and took a sip. The coffee was pretty strong, but he'd be okay.

He just needed to get away from Taylor for a bit.

But thank God for smart phones—the perfect invention to look like you weren't actually alone, that you were actually quite busy. He got on Facebook. Four people had "liked" the status he had posted earlier, "Microwavable pizza = let's heat up a plate of regret." The four "likes" provided a feeling similar to four brief pats on the back, before Andy started scrolling through his news feed to find something else to pacify him. Multiple people had posted cat pictures, two had posted links to a quiz entitled, "Which Star Wars Character Are You?," three had posted pictures of their kids on swing sets or other play equipment, while several others had posted their thoughts on recent news stories, "When will the president actually act presidential for a change?" "Why Hallman wasn't fired is a mystery greater than the Big Bang Theory." "Every plastic bottle thrown in the trash is an 'eff-you' to the planet. Straight and simple."

Andy, quickly bored with this, put his phone back in his pocket.

"Do you . . . watch a lot of TV?" the college-aged guy at the next table said to a girl sitting across from him.

"Some," she said. "Though most is so inane I can't sit through it."

"I agree."

"Do . . . *you* watch a lot of TV?"

"Some," the guy said. "Mmm-hmm. Some."

"What about Netflix?"

"Some."

"Me too."

Andy sat back, staring into space, wishing he had headphones or could move to another table without seeming rude.

He pulled out his phone to take another hit on the phone crack pipe, but instead of scanning Facebook, Instagram, or other social media options, he opened a "Note." He did still need to work on his speech for the funeral. Maybe he could jot down a couple ideas. But still, nothing came to mind that didn't sound trite or greatly exaggerated. *Model citizens. Perfect examples for their friends and family. Just always put others before themselves. Leaving behind a tremendous legacy.*

His parents had been nice, good people, but *give me a break—*

"The voter turnout was very low," the guy said.

"Because people feel helpless, I think," the girl said.

"Fourteen percent last election."

"Really?"

"I think. Though that was just a school board election, but still, just bad."

"Oh. Okay."

Andy looked up at the couple, wanting to give them some sort of hand, offer a few suggestions of things to talk about, ways to get more of a conversation going, even though he was by no means an expert. Maybe they just needed alcohol to lubricate things. Caffeine probably only raised nerves, anxiety—amplified any awkwardness.

But alcohol couldn't solve *everything*, Andy knew.

Still, as he snuck peeks at the girl and the guy, he felt a twinge of jealousy too. That even though this first date—God, he *hoped* it was a first date—seemed to be faltering, soon to sputter out and be pronounced dead on arrival, just the fact these two people were on one and he wasn't, filled him with envy.

So it had been a while . . . he had been busy . . . he was "working on himself" . . . working nights was the trouble . . . you could only date so much before you wanted to throw your hands in the air and say "fuck this!" . . . dating could be expensive—emotionally expensive too . . . he just had other priorities . . . but. . . .

He scanned the coffee shop, the beatnik barista bobbing his head to the psychedelic music, while the flyers on the bulletin board wafted thanks to the nearby ceiling fan spinning like a table saw.

The flyers. "Soul Smash" at Double Drive. Tonight.

There would likely be people of the female sex there.

Alcohol and females to sooth loneliness, frustration.

Andy drained the rest of his coffee, conquering the remaining half glass in one swoop, the coffee's acidity shoving its fist into his stomach, hitting him deep. He winced. He coughed and cleared his throat.

"I tried playing guitar for a couple months," the girl said. "Then I quit."

"Yeah, I quit the guitar too."

"Hey," Andy said.

They looked over, startled.

"Sorry, don't mean to butt in, but do you guys know where the Double Drive is? I've never been there."

"Oh," the guy said. "We're pretty close. It's just a couple blocks . . . that way, I think." He pointed. "On Tower Street by the 7-Eleven."

"Cool. Okay . . . yeah, I think I can find that. Thanks. There's a DJ playing soul music tonight. Thought I might check it out."

"Oh yeah? I like soul music," the girl said, perking up.

"You do?" the boy said.

"Yeah. That sounds fun," she said.

"Awesome," Andy said. "Well, you guys are obviously welcome to go too."

The guy and girl traded surprised looks like this was a novel idea—*they could go too.*

Andy rose to his feet, staggering slightly. "Well, thanks for the directions. Have a good night."

He left out the door, heading down Adams to Park. He knew exactly where Double Drive was and had been there dozens of times. The guy wasn't exactly right in his directions either, but that hadn't been the point in asking.

He soon arrived at Double Drive but not before coming under the sights of a homeless woman standing near the curb.

"Hey, can you help me out? Just a dollar?"

She had a cardboard sign, one of Andy's dad's particular pet peeves. "I get where they get the cardboard—stealing it out of a dumpster," Walter frequently said, "but where do they get the black marker? Tell me that one. Or is that what they give them at homeless shelters: markers for hassling people?"

Andy shook his head *no* and kept walking.

"Okay, God bless you," the woman said, keeping her head down.

Andy entered Double Drive, flashed his ID, and paid the three-dollar cover charge, and then made a beeline for the bar. On the list of drink specials was one called "the Double Drive Overdrive," which sounded pretty dorky, but it piqued his interest enough.

"Hey," Andy said, leaning over to the bartender, a female who, visually at least, was a perfect candidate for perhaps easing his loneliness, that is, if female bartenders weren't already so inundated with guys hitting on them already that it made you pathetically cliché to even try. "What is the Double Drive Overdrive?"

"It's Old Overholt rye, espresso, bitters, chartreuse, and some amaretto."

"Yeah, okay, I'll do that."

She quickly grabbed assorted bottles, flipping them upside down as their contents splashed into a rather small glass, the whole thing looking haphazard and rushed, but that was the way Andy liked it—there was something appealing, for some reason, about bartenders who looked distracted and in a hurry, bartenders who were like Jackson Pollock in their carefree throwing around of liquids rather than the bartenders who carefully measured out ingredients, making you a drink that was uniform and predictable.

After placing two small straws in the drink, she stirred it around, and then handed it to Andy who gave her a ten-dollar bill.

Andy took a sip. It was pretty tasty, but then the aftertaste hit, jabbing him in the back of the throat. He held the drink away from his mouth, his tongue stinging at the bitterness of it all. Well, not every Jackson Pollock painting was a masterpiece. He sipped on it again as he headed over to a table to sit by himself, figuring, well, maybe he could grow to like the taste. He had paid nine dollars plus tip for it.

Andy crossed his legs and looked over the room. About twenty or thirty people were sitting or standing in groups. The DJ on stage, a black guy with dreads, was in fact playing soul music, nodding to the beat as he placed a record on one of the turntables. The music sounded good, but the dance floor was still at an awkward number, ten or so people—not enough for a lone guy to go out there without looking like a weirdo.

In the corner, the door guy was mopping up a spill.

It was the first Thursday in a long time that Andy had been out and not working. It was pretty shitty that it took his parents dying for him to get a Thursday night off—but then again, he hadn't exactly been asking for Thursdays off—but his mood was already improving.

The song changed to something by, Andy was guessing, James Brown. All the grunted "Yeah!" "Ow!" "Ungh!" at least sounded like him, as if James had forever been poked in the side while recording his vocal tracks.

Andy turned his attention to a group of girls on the dance floor. Two or three were pretty attractive, cute faces, nice bodies, making it hard for him to look away. The jealousy he had felt at the Golden Cup soon switched over into a low simmer of lust, urging him to do *something*. But what was he going to do? Step over there and try to weasel into their group? He didn't want to be *that* guy, even if he had unfortunately been that guy several times. And certainly the ridiculousness of chasing ass on his first night in town for his parents' funeral did not escape his attention either. Still, it would be nice to have a little fun while he was here instead of just slogging down memory lane with his brother the whole time. The plans for the rest of the trip were one bummer after another: looking over things at their parents' house, the funeral, a post-funeral reception with family members—all designed to further accentuate the sadness of his parents' deaths, even though his own emotions were still rather numb about the whole thing.

The group of girls—probably mid-twenties— giggled about something and then motioned to another girl sitting by herself, ten feet away, who smiled and gave a single wave but remained seated, leaning her head against the wall.

Andy looked her over. Not exactly beautiful, maybe a little plain actually, but not bad, and inside he felt a pull to talk to her that didn't just seem like his dick doing the talking. She just looked sad. Like she was being left out.

He looked at his drink, which he quickly sucked down, his throat and stomach flinching the whole time.

He stood up and headed her way. His nerves prickled as he got closer, his heart rate picking up in tempo, the girl's face coming clearer into view—he had to think of something clever to say. Being an even moderately attractive girl—actually, just being a girl—meant you were likely accosted by creeps non-stop, so half the challenge of being a heterosexual man was trying to distance yourself from others—trying to come off as normal and not pathetic or desperate, even though deep down desperation was sewn into your DNA and not going anywhere.

"Hey, so," he said. She turned to him. "I know this is totally random, but I'm gonna get another drink. You, you want one? Oh, but don't choose the Double Drive Overdrive. It really sucks."

She let out a single "Ha," and then placed her hand over her mouth as if stopping something. "Oh, no thanks. Thanks though."

"Really? I don't mind. You don't have to talk to me all night or anything." He cut himself off. *God*, he sounded like a moron. Girls say they like a man with confidence, but all it takes is talking to one for the confidence to just leak right out. Drip, drip, drip.

The DNA strand for desperation is long and unwieldy.

"I'm actually not feeling that well," she said. She did look rather pale, a hint of sweat on her forehead. There was no drink, not even an empty glass, at her table.

"Really?"

"I think I got food poisoning or something."

"Oh shit. I've been pretty *ugh* today too."

She gave him a *bullshit* look.

"No, seriously," Andy said. He grabbed a nearby chair and pulled it up to her table. "Mind if I . . . ?"

She appeared to debate over her answer before saying, "Yeah, okay."

"Cool," Andy said, sitting down. He placed his empty Double Drive Overdrive on the table.

"Better not sit too close or you'll catch it."

"Food poisoning?"

"Ha. Never mind."

"Me," Andy said, "I got about two hours of sleep today, so I've been drinking a lot of coffee, which often makes my stomach pretty, y'know, *blah*, like it's pissed at me or something. But I need caffeine, and soda's not enough. And really bad for you, obviously."

"Coffee doesn't agree with you?" She looked intrigued. "Me neither. Even lattes and sugar-buried things, like at Starbucks. Every time I tempt it, like, maybe I've finally grown out of it, I'm reminded the answer is no."

"I can handle those basically okay a lot of times, but straight coffee, not as much. And the dinner I had with my brother and his wife—bad idea, yet so good in the moment—the food, I mean."

"What'd you eat?"

"Pasta. A lot of bread too. At . . . um, I forget the name. I couldn't pronounce it anyway. But I guess that's the point: if you're unable to pronounce it, it's immediately considered 'better' or 'fine dining.' "

"Well, you probably just ate too many carbs. The bad kind."

"Yeah," Andy said. "So what did you in?"

"A hamburger, I think. I know, boring, boring."

"No shame in that."

"It was locally raised too, which I guess is supposed to be good? I feel bad enough eating animals, but now I have to accept this one was once a neighbor."

Andy laughed. This girl was funny.

"I'm trying to cut out meat, but it's tough," she said. "But yeah, coffee and caffeine in general, I just avoid. I haven't had any in, like, six months."

"Really? How are you not, like, falling asleep all the time? Just hating everything?"

She leaned forward. "Lots and lots of cocaine."

They both laughed.

"No," she said, still looking a little weary and sick but also like she was happy to talk to someone. "One twenty-minute nap after work, eight hours of sleep every night, and then exercise. Nothing crazy, just normal stuff. But seriously, try giving up caffeine. When I did, I was really scared at first— like, *oh no*, how will I survive—but I soon noticed I was a lot less tired. I know it sounds crazy. But try it."

"Wow," Andy said, sitting back. "That does, that does actually scare me, ha, the idea of just giving it up."

"See, you have a drug problem. That's what caffeine is."

Andy smiled at her. "Where's caffeine rehab when you need it?"

She grinned and then the table suddenly fell silent like someone had pressed the mute button.

In the background, a song, maybe something by The Supremes?, played.

Andy looked at his empty drink. What . . . okay, what could they talk about now? It seemed a little overkill to continue talking about the negative effects of food and drinks, well, unless she wanted to, but she appeared done, once again back to her slouched, pale, slightly-sick self.

"Well, sure you don't want a drink?" Andy finally said. "I'm gonna get one. I could get you something light."

He stood up.

"I better not," she said.

"Oh." He couldn't say, "Well then never mind," and sit right back down, so he stepped away from the table, feeling slightly defeated.

Still, when he ordered his next drink—just a beer—telling himself to just give up on the girl before he made a complete ass of himself, he asked for a water too.

He walked back to her table, repeating a mantra in his head: *don't be creepy, don't be creepy, don't be creepy*. There was a fine line between sweet and creepy.

"Hey," he said, catching her attention again. "I got you this."

He slid the water her way.

She smirked. "How do I know you didn't drop some roofies in here?"

"No, I would never—"

"I'm just kidding."

Andy took a seat again, not sure if he were overstepping his bounds or not.

"I did slip some caffeine in there though," he said.

She smiled and took a sip of the water. Andy drank from his beer.

"Are those"—he pointed to the girls on the dance floor—"your friends?"

"Sort of."

"Kind of shitty of them to just leave you here alone."

"Well, I don't know them super well actually, but they all wanted to hang out. I'm in town for a wedding on Saturday. I'm one of the bridesmaids. I should just leave, but one of those girls out there is my ride, though I think she's kind of drunk. You're from here?"

"Originally, yeah, but I live in Kansas City now. Yeah, yeah, I know. No one knows anything about Kansas City."

"Ha, you're right. I don't think I've ever been there. Maybe driven through it."

"It's not exactly a big tourist place. They make a big deal out of the so-called famous BBQ there, which is pretty good, I guess, but nothing that special."

"Ugh. I think if I had any BBQ right now, I would . . . yeah, that wouldn't be good."

"Yeah, I kind of feel like not eating anything either for a very long time." He raised his glass. "To feeling shitty when you're out of town."

They clinked glasses.

"I'm Andy by the way."

"Shannon."

They kept talking from there, learning about each other. She was twenty-five and an interior designer in San Francisco, a job she described as getting to see the lives of rich people, without being rich herself. She and the bride, Rebecca, had gone to high school together in Madison, Wisconsin, a place she missed for its low cost of living (at least compared to San Francisco) and small community feel—but not the freezing winters.

They were sharing their thoughts on pets—she similarly found cats pretentious—when Andy's phone vibrated.

"Sorry, let me just see who this is." He took his phone out, seeing it was a text from Taylor. He noticed the time. It was past midnight.

Dude, where are you?? Do the right thing and come home now.

"Ah, it's nobody," Andy said, putting it back in his pocket.

He had said nothing to Shannon about why he was in town.

Some of the bridesmaids stumbled over.

"Whoa, who's this?" one said.

"I'm just some stranger, bugging your friend," Andy said, smiling. He took a sip from his drink, his fourth or fifth of the night, while Shannon had stuck to water.

"Did he just say that?"

"Look at Shannon, reeling 'em in," one of them, clearly wasted, said.

Shannon said, "No, we're just—"

"You two should come dance," another said.

Andy looked to the dance floor, which now had twenty or twenty-five people. He spotted an awkward-looking dude, maybe thirty-five, shirt buttoned all the way to the top, skittishly bopping his arms up and down like a marionette. He appeared alone. Behind him Andy saw—*wait*, it was the couple from the Golden Cup, dancing equally awkward but together, laughing and grinning at each other. Andy smiled. He hadn't seen them come in.

Andy turned to Shannon. "You want to? I think I could—"

"I'm still not feeling too well. I kind of just want to sit," Shannon said.

"Nope," one of the girls said, pulling Shannon, who shakily shot to her feet.

"Hey, easy," Andy said, reaching out as if to catch her.

"Okay, just for a little bit," Shannon said, frowning.

Andy joined her on the dance floor, as she began lightly moving to the music. She was less than a graceful dancer. Andy started moving as well, while leaning toward Shannon's ear. "We can go sit down if you want. I can fight them off. I deal with wasted bridesmaids all the time at the hotel. Something about being a bridesmaid makes them think they're invincible."

"What?" she yelled over the music.

"If you want to sit down," Andy said louder, "we can. I can tell them."

"No, that's okay. I think I can probably—oh. *Oh*—"

"What? You okay?"

Shannon stopped in place and leaned over, resting her hands on her knees, her body rocking forward and backward as if she were standing on a boat.

Her mouth moved, and she put her hand to her face.

Andy placed his palm on her back and spoke up, "Here, let's go—"

But it was too late as she began vomiting, it bypassing her thin fingers and landing on the floor in front of them, as well as Andy's shirt, a brown and maroon plaid button-down he had tonight, like always, worn with the top two buttons undone—his favorite shirt, the shirt he only allowed himself to wear once a week to avoid it appearing too frequently in his shirt rotation, despite his preference for it. At least he had left his gray jacket at their table.

"Oh!" one of the girls said.

"Oh no. *Sweetheart!*" another said.

Andy recoiled, his fingers clenching, but he held still.

More and more people began looking over.

"Oh, I'm so . . . sorry," Shannon said, still swaying, looking like she might do an encore.

"Are you gonna clean that up?" one of the bridesmaids said.

"Keely, shut up," another bridesmaid said. She came over and put her hands on Shannon's shoulder. "Let's get you to the bathroom."

The bridesmaid led Shannon, still hunched over, to the bathroom.

Andy stood there on the dance floor, lost on what to do.

The door guy came over with a mop, frowning at Andy.

Andy went to the men's room, chastising himself for being such a dumbass. What the fuck was he doing? What, was he gonna try to hook up with some sick chick? Were his desperation levels just that off the charts tonight?

He grabbed a handful of paper towels and wiped at his shirt, which seemed to get most of Shannon's vomit off him, or at least dampen it to a point close enough to extinction. Still, the shirt was probably fucked. Maybe he could order another one. It was a really nice shirt. Or *had* been. Then he washed his hands as he looked himself over in the mirror, continuing his frustrated internal dialogue. Bar bathroom mirrors were made for these kinds of things, these "You got this, man" or "What the hell are you doing?" Staring yourself in the face, sticking it to yourself. Pumping yourself up or tearing yourself down a peg.

He left the bathroom and saw the front exit, where he knew he should head. It wouldn't be fleeing. The girl was sick, incapacitated. What was he going to do? Administer antibiotics to her? Hook an IV up to her? Monitor her vitals? She had the bridesmaids, who, though they were pretty drunk and obnoxious, could take care of her, hail her a cab at least.

But instead he took a seat at their table. He grabbed his jacket but didn't put it on. There was still something about her he liked, beyond her biological designation as "female."

He looked down at his phone. It was nearly 1:00, and there was a fresh text from Taylor.

Seriously, where are you?? Are you dead?? This is so not cool!

Andy shook his head. In some ways, Taylor was right, but in other ways, Andy just wanted to tell him to fuck off and that he'd be home whenever he felt like it. He was in no mood to be chastised by his insufferable brother.

He was about to type back when a shaky voice said, "You're still here."

He looked up to see Shannon standing before him.

"Oh hey," Andy said, standing up. "How are you feeling?"

"I'm a little better, but I'm going to go."

"Yeah. That's probably a good idea."

"Keely's gonna take me back to the hotel. I feel bad about ruining their fun—yours too."

"Well, then let me take you," Andy said. "Seriously. No funny business. I'm not really that into vomit anyway."

"Well . . . okay."

Shannon limped over to the bridesmaids to say goodbye, them drunkenly embracing her, squeezing her neck with probably too much affection. Keely looked over Shannon's shoulder, eying Andy.

Shannon came back, and they headed out the front door into the brisk Chicago night. Shannon was shivering; so was Andy.

Andy took off his jacket and draped it around her.

"Oh thanks."

"Sure. Let's try to get a cab. The train might take too long."

"Excuse me," a voice called out.

Andy turned to see the homeless woman from earlier. She approached them while still keeping her distance.

"I'm sorry to bother you," she said, "but I would be so grateful for just a dollar. Anything. I'm trying to get to Detroit to my family. Please. Please." Her eyes were large, pleading.

Andy normally would've said *sorry* and quickly moved on, but with Shannon next to him, he said, "Okay," and then reached into his pocket and pulled out a dollar bill, handing it to the woman's cold hands.

"Oh, thank you! Thank you!" She smiled, feebly. "Could I, could I please get just another dollar? Please. It would help me so much."

An anger stirred up inside Andy. See, this was why you didn't get involved with homeless people. No one should have to be homeless, of course, but panhandling, taking advantage of people's generosity . . . it was like getting a Christmas present and then saying to the giver, "Thanks. Now what else ya got for me?"

Andy felt cornered. "Well . . . okay." He looked in his wallet, seeing the only other bills he had were twenties. "Sorry, I don't have another dollar. I—well . . . okay, I guess."

He grabbed a twenty-dollar bill and handed it to her.

Her eyes grew, her hands practically shaking.

"Oh my god! Thank you! Thank you!"

"Sure, sure."

He felt robbed. Angry. It was good doing something nice for someone else, and losing twenty dollars—or twenty-*one* rather—was no serious loss, but still, the nerve of that woman, taking advantage of his kindness. The whole Detroit story had probably been pure bullshit too. And if her family cared so much about her, why didn't *they* spring for a bus ticket for her? Why was it up to strangers you hassled outside of a bar to fund your supposed trip?

Out of the corner of his eye, Andy saw a cab coming down the street. He quickly thrust his hand in the air. The cab driver spotted them and pulled over to the curb.

Andy led Shannon to the door, holding it open for her.

"God bless you! Bless you!" the homeless woman called out.

Andy nodded and helped Shannon into the car, and then himself, closing the door behind them. He helped Shannon put her seatbelt on.

"That was really nice," Shannon mumbled, slurring her words, "what you did for that woman. You're, you're a nice guy."

"Thanks."

"She sick?" the cab driver said, eying them in the rearview mirror.

"A little."

"She better not puke in my car. Seriously, man."

"Just relax."

"No, I'm serious. No puking. She barfs and you two are out of here."

"Just fucking relax. If she does, I'll clean it up." The guy was a fucking cab driver at night, for God's sake. His job was cruising the bars looking for people unable to drive home or even walk to the nearby train or bus stops. Vomit and other bodily fluids were a natural consequence of his business, like crumbs on the floor of a restaurant.

The cab driver angrily gripped the steering wheel, shaking his head. "Fine, man. Don't make me regret this."

"So where's your hotel?" Andy asked Shannon.

"The Premiere on Millennium Street."

"The Pre*miere*?" Andy said. "Why would you stay there? They're so shitty. They're—" He cut himself off.

The cab driver screeched away from the curb, throwing Andy and Shannon around, despite their seatbelts.

"Hey, take it easy," Andy said.

The driver glared in the rearview mirror.

Shannon leaned onto Andy's shoulder.

"I'm just doing this for comfort. Don't get excited."

"That's okay," Andy said. He was tempted to put his arm around her, to pull her closer, but he kept his hands to himself. He didn't want to screw this up.

When they got to the Premiere, Shannon fumbled with the cab door for several seconds before finally getting it open. Andy got out too.

"Oh no, you don't have to," Shannon said.

"No, I don't mind. I'll just make sure you get in safely."

Andy paid the driver and leaned into the car. "See. Barf-free."

"Yeah, yeah."

They walked toward the sliding glass doors. There was a sign on the corner of the glass that said "No Smoking within 20 Feet of Door," which someone was clearly violating, standing by a rosebush maybe five feet from the door, sucking on a cigarette. They need to better enforce this, Andy thought. He wouldn't let that fly at the Stoddard. Similarly there were smudges on the sliding glass doors, particularly odd since those kind of doors didn't require anyone to touch them in the first place—why hadn't someone cleaned those off?

Inside the hotel a vacuum was standing next to a plant like it was hiding. No maintenance person appeared to be nearby, so what the hell was a vacuum doing there? Andy shook his head. This place should at least act like they give a crap. As they walked toward the elevator, Andy saw the person working the front desk texting on his phone. Couldn't people get off their fucking phones for one second, especially at work?

"This place is terrible," Andy mumbled as they entered the elevator.

"I forgot you work . . . in a hotel," Shannon said, still swaying while holding onto the wall in the elevator as it began its ascent.

"Yeah. I think I care too much," Andy said. "I might take some Windex to the front doors when I leave."

"Let me give you this before I forget," Shannon said, handing Andy's jacket back to him.

When the doors opened on her floor, the eleventh, Andy put his arm around her to keep her upright.

"Ugh," Shannon said. "I'm so sorry you have to see me . . . ugh . . . like . . . this."

They arrived at her door. She fumbled in her purse for her key card.

"Listen," she said, "nothing is going to happen between us."

"I know. Don't worry."

She dropped her key card and bent over to pick it up, Andy inadvertently catching a glimpse of her black underwear.

She opened the door and let him inside. The single bed was unmade with a bra dangling over a chair.

"Oh, Jesus. I didn't know anyone would see this."

She quickly grabbed the bra and shoved it in her suitcase. She then plopped on the bed, moaning.

"Just stay there," Andy said.

He walked into the bathroom and flipped on the light. Instinctually he looked around, assessing the layout and presentation, but the counters were covered with Shannon's makeup, moisturizers, cleansers, and more.

He reminded himself to focus, focus, but still he found himself counting the number of towels and complimentary items in the bathroom. He leaned down to the bar of hand soap by the faucet and smelled it, curious what kind of scent it was. Similarly, was it the kind of soap that left your hands refreshed or just sticky, like cheap hotels? Maybe he'd even wash his hands and find out—

"What are you doing?" Shannon said.

Andy jerked upright. "Oh. Nothing."

He grabbed one of the paper cups and filled it with water from the tap. He also grabbed the bathroom trashcan, and brought both out to Shannon, placing the water on her nightstand and the trashcan nearby on the floor.

"Oh. Thanks."

She crawled under the sheets, pulling the comforter up to her chin, but she was still shivering. Andy walked to the closet, and before he could inspect the meager offerings or count the number of hangers for comparison to the Stoddard, he grabbed the extra blanket and brought it over and placed it on her.

She grinned. "You're too nice."

"I do this for a living—well, not *this*, but you know. . . . So how are you feeling? Still cold? Too hot?"

"Still a little cold, I guess."

He walked over to the thermostat and bumped up the temperature two degrees, before returning to her and squatting down so he was at eye level. He placed his hand on the part of the blanket on her shoulder.

"Despite you being sick and all, you seem pretty cool. I'd like to see you again. I'm here for the weekend, and so are you."

"I guess we could do that. You're being really nice. I'm still waiting for things to turn."

"I'll try to be meaner next time to balance the scale."

She smiled, and when Andy pulled out his phone, she recited her phone number, which he entered into his phone under the name "Shannon San Francisco."

He rose to his feet and patted her on the shoulder.

"Good night," he said.

"Good night."

Taylor hadn't given him a key, so when Andy arrived at the front door of the apartment around 2:30 a.m., he called his brother, who in a sleepy huff unlocked the door and let him in.

"One drink, huh?" Taylor said, wearing gym shorts, black socks, and a t-shirt that said *Milwaukee Racquet Club Association*. "How big was this drink? Like a keg?"

"Shut up. Whatever. I was helping a girl get home."

They walked inside Taylor and Candice's apartment, the living room lit only by a lamp.

" 'Helping her get home.' Jeez. This is what I was talking about," Taylor continued in his shouty whisper. "Well, while you were having fun, Candice and I inflated the mattress for you."

"Oh. Thanks. I could've—"

"Just go to sleep. We're leaving at 8:00. Glad you got your rocks off."

" 'Rocks off'? Do you realize how old you sound? And nothing like that happened."

Taylor shook his head, flipped off the lamp, and stepped down the hall to his bedroom, closing the door behind him.

Andy sat on the mattress, which immediately depressed a little under him. He took off his shoes and jacket, changed out of his vomit-stained shirt, and pulled the collection of sheets and blankets over his body, the air mattress wobbling underneath him like a bouncy house for kids, he the adult upsetting the balance. Similarly, the room was slightly spinning. *God*, he was kind of drunk. But mostly he was thinking, as he had been the entire walk home, about Shannon.

5

Andy woke up for what had to be the third or fourth time.

He changed positions, the air inside the mattress ebbing and flowing like he was on a waterbed. He grabbed his phone off the nearby coffee table, hoping to see a text or something from Shannon, but there was, of course, nothing. Instead, he saw the time flashing back at him: 3:50 a.m. He had barely slept over an hour. And 3:50 . . . this was the time he was normally at work.

He lay back on the mattress, his back aching slightly. He closed his eyes, trying to will himself to sleep, but there was a subtle anxiety tapping at him.

Tap.

Tap.

Tap.

He reached out and grabbed his phone and pressed the button for the Stoddard.

He counted the number of rings before the call was answered.

"The Stoddard in Kansas City, this is William speaking."

I LOOK LIKE YOU

The way the greeting was delivered—and two rings before being answered: perfect. William, one of the good ones.

"Will, hey, it's, it's Andy."

"*Andy*! Hey, man. What's—aren't you out of town?"

"Ha, yeah," Andy said, seeming to suddenly realize how preposterous his calling was. "I'm not drunk or anything. Nope, nope. Just thought I—well, everything going okay?"

"Sure. Pretty slow night. No mishaps or anything." In William's voice, Andy could hear the sound of shrugging. "Slow, man. Everything, everything okay with you?"

Was that—Andy heard what sounded like a sputter, a lisp.

"Are you chewing gum?" Andy said.

"Oh—woops, yeah. Sorry. Here, let me . . . okay, just tossed it in the trash. Sorry."

"Cool, thanks. Ha. Don't mean to manage you from five-hundred miles away, but, y'know."

"Oh yeah. Sorry. My bad."

The line fell silent.

"So," William said. "Anything else I can do for you?"

"Um . . . so Erin's managing tonight, right?"

"Mmm-hmm."

"And everything's going fine?"

"Sure. Going great."

He was almost disappointed to hear. Like what, the whole hotel would go to shit with him gone for one night? And he was regularly gone two nights a

83

week! He didn't work every single night. So what if Erin was normally a daytime manager; it didn't mean she couldn't—

"Oh," Andy finally said.

"Everything okay?" William said.

"No—I mean, yeah, yeah, just . . . ha . . . sorry, maybe I *am* a little tipsy still. Sorry, man. Well, cool. Good talking to you."

"Yeah, sure. You . . . you too."

"Night, dude," Andy said.

He set the phone on the table, mortified, and lay back on the mattress, the whole thing swaying a bit. He pulled the blankets up over his chin and closed his eyes tightly, tightly, until he eventually drifted into some semblance of sleep.

6

"All right. Up. Up."

Andy's eyes slowly opened to see Taylor standing over him, fully dressed, holding a coffee mug.

"Come on," Taylor said, further lowering his gaze.

"Shhh," Candice said from the kitchen, where she was running the sink.

"It's 7:30," Taylor said. He drummed his fingers on the coffee mug.

"But you . . . you said," Andy squeaked out. He cleared his throat, grabbed at his forehead, which was aching with the effects of a hangover. "You said we were leaving at 8:00."

"What'd you do to the mattress?"

Andy, eyelids still at half-mast, peered past the disarrayed pile of blankets surrounding him, the blankets looking like he had challenged them to a kick-boxing match during the night, and saw what Taylor was talking about: the air mattress had mostly deflated. He was lying practically on the floor.

Andy groaned and kicked off the rest of the blankets, and slowly rose, taking a moment to find his footing.

In the shower, Andy remembered the phone call only a few hours before. He let out a chuckle at his behavior, *calling my work like that!*, but it tapered off quickly.

Well. . . .

So I care about my job a whole lot—so what?

It just so happens I take my work very seriously.

When you're single, you take your work more seriously—have to find a place to put your attention, care. Your focus.

Got to care about something.

Well—

It was when several minutes had passed and he heard Taylor knocking on the door, saying, "It's almost 8:00," that Andy snapped to attention, realizing he had been soaping his genitals for probably a solid five minutes, his dick fully erect, seemingly looking up at him in confusion.

"Just a minute!"

Taylor drove the three of them to their parents' house thirty minutes away. Andy squirmed in the backseat like a child unable to hold still. He still felt like shit—dehydrated, achy—and for some reason Taylor had the A.C. cranked, making the car freezing.

"Did you know I had to identify the bodies?" Taylor said.

"Oh," Andy said, squinting and rubbing at his head once again. "I'm sorry you had to do that." Andy coughed. Scratched the back of his head. "How was it?"

"Well, imagine seeing your dead parents on a table, their faces mangled. Yeah."

"Okay, okay," Andy said. "I said I'm sorry—"

"Taylor, their faces weren't mangled," Candice said, almost sheepishly, the first thing she had said in probably fifteen minutes.

"What are you talking about?" Taylor said.

"Their faces weren't mangled. They looked peaceful, if anything. Their faces were fine, except for the cut on your dad's forehead. It was their torsos that . . . y'know, had the most damage, apparently, but"—she made eye contact with Andy in the rearview mirror—"they didn't show us that. We just had to see their faces."

"Yeah, well—" Taylor said.

"It was still very sad," Candice said.

As they pulled up to a stoplight, Taylor peered toward his wife, squinting, and said, almost in a whisper, "What are you doing?"

"I'm just telling the truth."

Taylor turned back to the road, and when the light switched to green, he hit the gas pedal with more oomph than normal, jerking them forward.

Taylor stuck the key in the lock and opened the front door. It was eerie stepping inside. In some ways, Andy still expected his mom to come around the corner, wiping her hands on a dishtowel, or his dad to greet them with something on his iPad he wanted to show. But no, it was predictably quiet, Candice, Taylor, and Andy walking in like trespassers to an abandoned museum. Andy had last been here on Christmas, where the four of them plus Candice had gathered in the living room, opening presents and drinking hot chocolate, the whole thing looking like an idyllic Americana scene. Moments earlier, Taylor and Andy's dad had done the same thing he had done their entire thirty years, going over to the Christmas tree with its gifts spilling out the bottom, and, peering around unsure, said, "Oh, let me see if Santa's been here . . . yes, yes, it looks like he has."

As they stepped farther into the house, Andy heard a light whirring sound, which after some looking around he realized was the DVR running, recording something. Without thinking twice, he pressed the power button, shutting it down. Elsewhere, the living room showed the effects of having been placed on pause. The newspaper from Monday was still on the table by their father's living-room chair. A few magazines and a blanket waited near the couch where their mom had usually relaxed in the afternoon.

In the kitchen, Andy saw some bills on the table. He assumed he and Taylor were now responsible for handling those, getting things shut off, accounts closed down—but he just didn't want to think about it yet.

Their dad's coffee mug was sitting on a placemat in front of the kitchen chair that had been "his" for as long as Andy could remember.

"This is so weird," Andy said.

"I know," Taylor said, calmly.

Andy picked up the mug.

"I was actually hoping to keep that," Taylor said.

"Oh. Yeah, sure," Andy said, handing it to Taylor.

"Or did you want it?" Candice said to Andy.

"No, no. It's okay."

Taylor fingered the cup in his hand. It was a simple blue and orange cup that said *Auburn*, their dad's alma mater.

Andy sat down in one of the kitchen chairs—but not his father's—and stared into space.

"Okay," Taylor said, snapping to attention. "I'm going to grab some boxes in the basement. Let's make some piles in the front hall. Anything you want to keep, just put it in your box. Any disputes, we'll work out. Candice can act as a mediator."

Andy scoffed at his brother's judiciousness.

"The rest," Taylor continued, "the company coming on Monday will deal with and sell."

"And we get some of this money?"

"Yes. After their fee."

"Wait," Andy said, "and what's happening to the house?" He hadn't even thought about that. There was, he was realizing, an endless list of things to do when someone died. Taking care of the body was maybe the least of it.

"We're selling it."

Andy frowned. He hadn't been consulted about any of this, but what would he have said anyway?

"You don't want it," Andy finally said.

"Well . . . it's in slight disrepair and just really outdated. I'd rather use the money for my tuition anyway."

Andy scoffed again. "Yeah. Whatever." And just what did Candice want, he wondered once more.

"You'll get your share from the sale."

Andy frowned. He didn't bother asking what percentage that would be. He could see Taylor giving himself a bigger share because he had taken care of the arrangements or because he had a wife and she should be entitled to some of it, or whatever. There was no such thing as a fifty-fifty split with Taylor.

Taylor headed to the basement to grab the boxes.

"You would've kept the house," Andy said to Candice.

She looked hesitant to respond. "It's a beautiful house."

"Mmm-hmm."

He was tempted to say "you deserve a beautiful house," but it sounded like something on a greeting card, so he kept his mouth shut, fumbling for something further to say, but then Taylor returned with two large boxes. He pulled a sharpie from his pocket, like he had planned for this all along, and wrote "Andrew" on one box and "Taylor" on the other.

"We can get more boxes if we need to," he said, capping the marker. He consulted his watch. "Damn, it's already 8:45. Okay, let's start with the living room. I give us about twenty or thirty minutes. That should be enough. Okay. Let's go."

Andy slowly rose to his feet and followed Taylor and Candice into the living room, where the three of them began going through things, thumbing through the bookshelves, looking through the modest DVD and VHS collection, glancing over the old turntable next to the stereo, both from the seventies, both with a thin sheet of dust over them.

From a top shelf, Taylor grabbed the wedding photo album from 1975. "Okay if I keep this?"

"Um. Yeah. Okay. Sure."

Taylor continued to grab various things, a porcelain dog, a box set of Abbott and Costello movies, a bookend that said *Auburn*, a landline phone—why, in the age of cell phones, he wanted to acquire a landline phone, Andy didn't know.

"You going to take any of the furniture?" Andy asked him. Their parents had nice living room chairs, tables, and lamps, things Andy didn't need but maybe Taylor's apartment could use. They definitely looked nicer than what Taylor and Candice had.

"Hmm. Nah, we're good," Taylor said, returning to the bookshelves.

Andy exchanged eye contact with Candice.

Really, he wasn't sure when his allegiance had switched from Taylor to mostly Candice. Though he had liked Candice from the beginning, he had, naturally, felt a stronger bond with his brother, no matter how many grievances they had with each other. They were brothers, after all. Twenty-plus years and then a new person shows up. But eventually he had found himself siding almost solely

91

with Candice, more concerned with her wishes and happiness than his brother's.

Even though Andy then moved to Kansas City. And didn't call much. Or email.

Even though he wasn't there, physically or even emotionally.

His brother, just an uptight crank, indignant when everyone else had a right to be indignant at him.

And it wasn't a single event that had made Andy cross party lines. It was gradual. Sometime in their mid-twenties perhaps. When more of Taylor's true self started showing, the self Andy had had glimpses of before but was now front and center, not only when Andy was around but also when Candice was.

Perhaps it was natural in any romantic relationship. You spend the first while being on your best behavior, being your best self, and after a while, something just relaxes or slips out.

It had happened in Andy's own relationships.

When maybe about nine months in, the both of them twenty-four, Andy told Liz Gardner he didn't feel like attending the upcoming charity fundraiser she was so excited about, even though he had "enthusiastically" gone to several with her before. When he finally admitted, and felt comfortable doing so, that he just saw them as rich people (or people wishing/pretending they were rich) showing up mainly for the photo-ops, playing like they actually gave a shit, while really just engaging in stuffy conversations or complaining about the hors d'ouevres, not cause they were *so, so, so* concerned about lupus.

Or a couple years ago, soon before he and Natalie Vanderveen broke up, when she moved in with him to see how living together went, that he started to notice she spent almost all her free time sitting on the couch, watching TV, painting and repainting her nails, almost always in the pajamas she rarely washed because she "wasn't a girl who smelled," while all the time before they had lived together, she had gotten dressed and acted excited to do things outside the home. And she wasn't just "a little depressed" or going through a phase. In fact, she seemed the opposite of depressed, peppering their conversations with enthusiastic vignettes about what was happening on _____ TV show or sticking her feet in Andy's face, giggling when he squirmed, inquiring again and again about what he thought of the aqua-blue tint on her toenails or whatever color she was into that week (feisty orange, simmering sunburst, passionate red, galactic green, etc.), and never believing him when he said it looked nice. And soon months of disagreements ended in a new agreement: that maybe living together was a mistake, or more specifically: maybe being together was a mistake. As their now true selves just didn't click.

Once they finished the living room and then the rest of the first floor, including the kitchen and garage, Taylor had filled one box and was halfway through a second, while Andy had taken nothing. His parents had some nice possessions, sure, but he wasn't dying to take home a bunch of electronics he didn't need, and most of the personal pieces just didn't mean as much to him as they apparently did to his brother. He didn't need his father's company golf trophy from 1995 or the portrait of their cousin Irene and her husband from her wedding a few years ago. Taylor even took an old black address book he found in a drawer—what he was going to do with that, Andy couldn't possibly imagine.

After a quick lunch, Taylor led them to the upstairs bedroom that he and Andy had shared until ninth grade, when the constant tug-of-war over who got which bunk bed or whose toy or CD belonged to whom made their parents finally give in to their repeated separate bedrooms plea. The room, in its current state, still had several of Taylor's things from childhood, a Smashing Pumpkins poster on the wall, a Frank Thomas autograph, some clothes, a few books.

"Haha!" Candice said, laughing at a framed photo of Taylor, Andy, and their dad in full camouflage outfits and face paint, a Halloween costume when the boys were nine. Their dad stood in the center, muscles flexed, looking like an army general, while the boys, soldiers, stood on either side of him, posing with serious faces and toy guns.

"Oh yeah, that's funny," Taylor said, taking it from her.

"You guys were so funny," Candice said.

Andy accepted the photo from Taylor, and looked it over. Despite his bad mood and persistent headache, he couldn't stop his lips from curling into a grin.

"That was such a bad idea for a costume," he said. "Our face paint rubbed off on everything. The camouflage legitimately worked. We almost got hit by so many cars that night."

Taylor held out his hand, ready to take it back.

Andy stared at the photo, warming to it even more. "I guess I could add this to my box."

Taylor dropped his hand. "Well . . . I mean, this is in my room. I should get it, right?"

Andy paused. "You've taken practically everything already. Why can't I just keep this one? This used to be my room too."

Taylor looked to Candice. "Well . . . I mean, it's mine, though."

Andy shoved the photo into Taylor's hand.

Candice stared at Taylor.

"What?" Taylor said. "It's *my* picture."

Andy considered pointing out they could just make a copy of the photo, but in some ways that wasn't the point.

"Whatever. I'll go start on Mom and Dad's room."

He walked down the hall, still feeling like Taylor was nothing but a whiney, selfish asshole, but when he stepped foot in his parents' room, this was replaced by the childlike thrill he had gotten anytime he had entered their room without their knowledge, as if he were a twelve-year-old again, hoping to find a *Playboy* or peek at a birthday present weeks before he was supposed to.

He looked around, taking it all in. The bed was perfectly made, the tan comforter pulled up to the six pillows—three for each of them. A book was resting on his dad's side of the bed. Andy stepped closer. *Night Fall* by Nelson DeMille. On his mom's side was a copy of *O* magazine, with, surprise, Oprah on the cover.

He started looking through his dad's dresser. In the top right drawer were a few small items he thought he might keep, such as his dad's old watch, a Rolex that had been a present from his grandfather upon graduating from Auburn. The watch was permanently dusty looking, and the battery had long ago died, plus it might seem a little gaudy actually wearing it, but it could be something to keep as a memento at least.

He then moved to his mother's nightstand and opened the single drawer, where he saw, mixed in with a bunch of recipes and pages torn out of magazines, a piggy bank. He grabbed it and shook it, the *cling-clang* of change reverberating in the tall-ceilinged room.

He turned it over but there was no way to get the change out without smashing the piggy bank to pieces.

He looked it over. There was nothing special or sentimental about this particular piggy bank—it was just a porcelain pig, probably from the eighties. And the change inside . . . they could just donate it to charity or something. Might as well.

Andy stepped out into the hall to look for the small toolkit his dad kept in the hall closet.

He overheard Taylor and Candice still in Taylor's room.

"Oh, look at these," Candice was saying.

"Oh yeah, my Ryne Sandberg cards. I don't know why I was so obsessed with him."

"You're still obsessed with him."

Andy found the toolkit and brought it into his parents' room, setting it on the bed. He pulled out the small hammer, set the piggy bank on the floor, and without a second thought, smashed it open.

"Whoa, everything okay in there?" Taylor called out from his room.

"Yep, just getting the money from Mom's piggy bank. We can donate it."

"Oh that's a good idea," Candice said.

Andy brushed away the broken porcelain, seeing a bunch of change, including a Kennedy half-dollar. Maybe he'd hold onto that. But then he also saw a piece of paper folded into a small square like a high school love note.

He picked it up, grinning. Probably just nothing, but he unfolded it and began reading.

Helen,

This weekend was just perfect. Don't feel bad for anything that happened. It was right. It's times like these that make me not feel so bored and unhappy. Not just another married guy staring down 50 more years of the same thing everyday. Something new and exciting for a change. Something good. I think you felt similarly. Until next time?

Yours,

Skip

Andy's grin faded, and his heart rate picked up. A chill passed down his back.

What the hell was this?

He looked at the corner of the letter, seeing a date written in rough, male handwriting: *February 9, 1983.*

He did the math: that was a little less than nine months before he and Taylor were born.

He sat back on the carpet, his body feeling woozy, his hangover beating like a bass drum on his head.

Skip . . . Skip . . . Skip . . . *Potter*? Skip Potter . . . an old family friend who lived, or at least used to, a few blocks from here. A frequent guest at his parents' parties. A nice man.

Oh.

Andy replayed all the memories he had of Skip Potter, but they were mostly unremarkable. Skip holding a glass of scotch and smiling. Skip playing badminton in the backyard with his wife and Andy's parents, while Skip's kids ran around with Taylor and Andy. He couldn't recall any behavior suggesting that something romantic had been going on . . . but maybe this had only happened before Andy and Taylor were alive or cognizant of anything strange.

Oh.

But yeah . . . he would always bring Taylor and Andy gifts, candy, baseballs, comic books, those kind of things, just out of the blue. Andy had just always assumed Mr. Potter was a nice guy, that he probably lavished similar gifts on his own kids.

Oh.

Oh.

The gross tang of bile climbed up Andy's throat. He swallowed and then lay back on the carpet, staring up at the ceiling. The room was slightly spinning, as if he were drunk all over again. He squinted and rubbed at his eyes. He breathed deeply.

Finally, he struggled to his feet and tiptoed down the stairs to his brother's boxes in the front hall.

He dug out the wedding album and there a few pages in, in a picture of the groomsmen, was Skip Potter, mustache, dark brown hair, his hands clasped in front of him like the other men. He had to be twenty-five or so when this was taken. Andy stared at the photo, his eyes nearly going cross-eyed from how intensely he was staring, his heart still racing. Skip at an age in the photo not much younger than Andy was now, and he *did* look a bit like Andy and Taylor.

Andy slammed the book shut and dropped it back in his brother's box.

Skip and their mom? But how could that be possible? She had always been a sweet woman, usually at home, quiet, reserved, seemingly content. She had been traditional and okay with it, situating herself in the kitchen or folding clothes in the laundry room, humming something inoffensive she had heard on the radio.

But—

Andy slowly padded up the steps, staring at his feet and running his hand up the banister.

"Hey. How are things going?"

Andy jumped, looking up to see Candice standing at the top of the stairs.

He pulled his hand back from the banister, shoving it in his pocket.

"You okay?" Candice said, her eyes narrowing.

"Oh. I'm just, you know, just hungover."

"Ha. Happens to the best of us. Want me to get you some water or Ibuprofen or something?"

"No, no, that's okay. Thanks." Man, it was like she would wait on him, hand and foot, if he asked. She was just so nice.

"Come on guys, we have a lot to do," Taylor called from his room.

"I think I'm . . . yeah," Andy said, "I'm going to get some coffee. That's what I need. You guys want anything?"

"Sure!" Candice said.

Candice told Andy what she'd like, followed by Taylor who acquiesced that he *guessed* it would be okay if Andy were gone for ten minutes.

"Okay. I'll be back in a few."

"Yeah, make it quick," Taylor called from his room. "You know, Candice could've grabbed you some coffee when she got lunch."

"You sure everything's okay?" Candice asked, turning her head to Andy.

"Yeah. Definitely. Just . . . yeah."

Andy headed out the front door, his legs feelings heavier than usual, and walked the few blocks to a coffee shop called the Grand Bean. Inside, he got in line. His phone was in his pocket, ready for his eyes to gaze at to kill time, but no, no, he didn't want to, so instead he just stuck his hands in his pockets, listening to the overhead music—The Strokes?—which seemed a little too loud, the uneasy feeling continuing, so he pulled out his right ring finger and stuck it in his mouth, chewing on the nail. It was a bad habit, for sure, but it was so satisfying when he could cleanly trim a nail using his teeth. So once the ring finger was done, he moved on to the others, doing his best to get a nice cut each time.

He had just finished his left pinky when he got to the front of the line.

"Hi," he said to the barista. "Okay, I—" A nail fragment slipped off his lips, landing on the counter near the tip jar. "Oh jeez, sorry."

He brushed it aside, the college-aged barista looking back at him with confusion.

"Um, can I get—it's gonna be three things, all to go—an Americano, and two soy lattes—all large. Oh wait." Shannon popped into his mind, their discussion about coffee, caffeine. "Um, well actually, instead of one of the soy lattes, can I. . . ." He looked over their list of juices. Maybe that would be a better, healthier option, less likely to anger his stomach. Maybe it was something he could tell Shannon about later. "Well, what would you recommend? For a juice?"

The girl perked up. "Oh! I personally love the Green Giant. It's mango, cilantro, spinach, coconut water, kale, agave nectar, goji berries, papaya, allspice, and acai."

"Wow."

"Oh and mustard greens."

"A lot of stuff," Andy said.

She leaned forward. "It really clears you out. Makes ya real regular!"

Though regularity wasn't his problem—in fact, he'd love to be irregular for a change—Andy said, "Okay, sure."

When the three drinks were ready, the barista put them in a cardboard drink caddy made out of eighty percent post-consumer recycled materials, something Andy wouldn't have noticed if it weren't printed in large type all over the caddy, like a child jumping up and down for its parents' attention.

Andy carried the drinks toward the exit but then veered off and took a seat at a table by the window. He didn't want to leave just yet, even though he had been gone over twenty-five minutes, perhaps messing up Taylor's hyper-detailed timetable.

He looked out the window, several people walking by, moving, in motion, progress, going forward. It was weird to be sitting still, watching other people moving by in a hurry.

He glanced down at his nails, all neatly trimmed.

He reached for the Green Giant, suddenly alarmed by just how large it was, not quite the same size as a Big Gulp but close enough.

Andy took a sip, the juice initially tasting pungent and strong, but then . . . *wait, this isn't bad.* He sipped again. And another time. It tasted . . .

really, it tasted great, refreshing, making him feel like less of an idiot for shelling out eleven dollars for this—eleven!—almost three times the price of the coffees. But maybe it was worth it, especially if it was so healthy—so healthy and delicious, beaming with taste and energy, that he almost forgot the note he had just uncovered, the whole reason he had fled to the Grand Bean in the first place.

The note.

He sighed, wondering if this was what he'd now feel this weekend instead of grief over his parents' deaths—betrayal, confusion, anger.

Skip Potter.

Andy hadn't seen him in probably fifteen years. He had been a regular fixture at the Canton house for a while but then had disappeared from his parents' social circle. What had happened? Maybe he had just moved away, or had Andy's dad found out about what had, seemingly, happened between his wife and Skip?

Oh.

"Dad" was possibly not their dad.

And why had his mom saved the note and put it in her piggy bank? It was hardly much of a love note, for one. And for a cheating guy—if that were the case—Skip was hardly discreet, leaving a paper trail like that. But Andy's mom was hardly discreet either, *saving* it.

Andy's sudden enthusiasm brought on by the Green Giant was wavering.

His phone buzzed with a text from his brother.

Where are you??

Andy texted back, seeing the time once again, *Sorry on my way!*

When Andy returned, he handed the coffees to Candice and Taylor at the top of the stairs. He had, nervously, as if anticipating something, drank about half the Green Giant on the walk back. So far he didn't feel an urge to use the bathroom.

"Thanks," Candice said.

"Eww, this is cold," Taylor said after taking a sip. "How far away did you go? You were gone like forty-five minutes."

"Sorry . . . I. . . ."

"Okay, what's wrong with you?" Taylor said. "Something happen last night?"

Andy took a deep breath and reached into his pocket, extracting the note and handing it to Taylor without a word.

Taylor read it over, brows furrowed, while Candice looked on too, her eyes growing when she got to the end.

Once he was done, Taylor glanced up at Andy.

"What is this?"

"I found it in mom's piggy bank. I think mom cheated on dad."

Taylor shook his head vehemently. "*What*? No, she wouldn't have done that. See, I *knew* you'd try to stir up trouble."

"I didn't make it up, dude."

"But I don't get it—"

"Do the math. That note's dated almost nine months before we were born, as in about the time we would've been conceived. Skip is probably Skip Potter."

Candice placed her hand over her mouth.

"Skip Potter." A look of recognition came onto Taylor's face.

"Who's Skip Potter?" Candice said, through her muffled mouth.

"He was a family friend," Andy said.

"No, no, I don't believe any of this," Taylor said, waving his hands. "Mom wouldn't have done that."

Andy hurried down the stairs to Taylor's boxes in the front hall, grabbed the wedding album, and carried it upstairs, opening it to the page that showed Skip Potter, groomsman number two.

"He *looks* like us," Andy said.

Taylor again waved his hands in the air. "So we're generic looking!"

"Come on."

"We look like half the WASPy people in America."

"He has blue eyes. We have blue eyes. Neither Mom nor Dad had blue eyes."

"That doesn't mean anything."

"Oh my god," Candice said, taking a step back.

"Now come on, we have a lot of work to get done," Taylor said. "It's—no, Mom wouldn't have done that, and that doesn't change that our *parents*—yes *our* parents, *OUR* parents—are dead." He kept shaking his head, almost violently. "Seriously—just, just, just *shut up!*" He threw his arms out, pushing Andy off-balance.

"Whoa—*fuck*," Andy said, as he started to tip over the lip of the top step.

Candice gasped and then reached out to grab his arm, gripping him tightly, as he swung against the wall next to the stairs, her grasp stopping him from falling down the steps. It would've been just a few feet at most, not a serious fall, but it was the fact that it had nearly happened.

Andy righted himself and regained his balance, finally planting his feet a step from the top.

"You almost pushed your brother down the stairs!" Candice shrieked.

"No—he—no, he was faking it. I hardly touched him." Taylor's eyes lit up like he was cornered.

"You are ridiculous," Andy said. "You can go through the rest of the house yourself. I don't want any of it anyway."

He hurried down the stairs, Candice calling after him, and when he left through the front, slamming the door behind him, he heard the sounds of Candice yelling at Taylor, Taylor apparently saying nothing.

7

Andy walked around the neighboring streets, shivering slightly in his gray jacket. As much of an asshole as Taylor could be, it was still hard to imagine he intended to push him down the stairs. Did he?

Andy walked a couple more blocks before taking a seat on a wooden bench in Watson Park, the bench free from pocketknife carvings or handwritten phone numbers and messages, the park similarly spotless, with well-manicured grass surrounding a play area containing wood chips and modern playground equipment, not the splinter-causing wooden jungle gyms of his childhood. He gazed at his left ring finger, as if expecting to find a splinter still there. He had gotten so many on that particular finger as a kid, from this very park, from the rickety equipment that used to be here.

He shoved his hands back in his jacket pockets, his fingers flexing and clenching against the mesh pockets, the height of the jacket's zipper now seeming nothing but trivial.

He turned to the swing set, where a woman about his age was pushing her daughter in the swing, the daughter's chubby legs kicking up and down in ecstasy, the woman pushing with one hand, while staring at a cell phone in her other hand.

Jesus! Andy wanted to yell. *Look at your daughter for once!*

Other people were walking dogs. Some people were pushing strollers. A father and his preschool-aged son were kicking a soccer ball back and forth.

Seemingly all the nearby people were tending to their dependents, the people and animals they cared for, while Andy only had himself.

He was thirty, but it still seemed like "Huh? Why?" when he saw people his age with kids. Why not live it up for a few more years before taking that plunge? He wanted to be a father someday . . . well . . . did he? But the piggy-bank note was a reminder there was always a slight hitch in fatherhood, a possible footnote, clarification, or retraction, that there was always a chance the child might not be yours, whereas a woman could be sure it was hers, save for some Lifetime movie-esque hospital switch. And if it was true that Skip was his father, and not the man he had called "dad" for his entire life, Andy didn't know with whom to be most upset. His mother for straying? Skip for tempting her? His "dad" Walter for not giving his wife what she wanted or needed?

It was even clearer now how little Andy Canton knew about his parents and their marriage.

And what encouragement did this give him to one day be a father himself? To not make him paranoid the whole time, to not make him insist on a paternity test like some daytime talk show?

In the case of one-year-old Brett . . . Andy, you are . . . not the father!

But if his mom hadn't strayed, he wouldn't even be alive.

And what was he supposed to take away from that consideration?

Andy pulled his shoulders up to brace against a cool gust of wind. He looked down again at the park bench, seeing someone had in fact defaced it with a small carving of either a penis or a handgun—it was hard to tell; they both could cause a lot of damage.

He looked back to the swing set, where the mom was now squatting in front of her daughter, taking a photo, the daughter still kicking merrily in the swing, despite it not moving. The mom then knelt beside her, putting her right arm around her child, while she held the phone in front of them to take a selfie.

Andy realized he was staring. He looked away. These days you couldn't be a man sitting in the park, supposedly just hanging out, without someone freaking out and calling the cops, so Andy pulled out his phone to at least look occupied before he decided what his next move would be—he would not be returning to his parents' house today. Or ever again. There was no reason to. Let Taylor continue swimming in his pool of nostalgia and the past. Andy just didn't care to. Nostalgia didn't fill him with the pleasant sensation it seemed to fill other people. It only reminded him of past failures that, even if in hindsight were "the right thing to do," still nagged at him.

The word for that was *regret*.

Maybe he could've learned to like the charity fundraisers Liz loved going to. *She* wasn't someone who pretended to be rich. *She* wasn't just feigning interest in whatever cause in order to get her picture in the paper, to feel "important." Maybe Natalie *had* been a little depressed, and maybe they could've worked at their issues and gotten past them.

The same with Heather, Val, Tori—all of them.

His parents too.

His parents.

The whole point of growing up is to eventually leave the nest, strike out on your own, be your own person, get *your* space, but the last part of the story is to someday come back, whether physically or just metaphorically.

He was supposed to one day visit his parents in a nursing home, help his dad find his coat, get groceries for his mom, take the endless bottles of pills and divvy them up into little piles, divided by day. Help ease the transition to the inevitable.

Andy sighed.

He should've—

"Oh!" he jumped when a man sat down next to him on the bench, awakening him from his daze.

"Oh, sorry," the elderly man said. "Just had to get off my feet for a second." A small dog on a leash, a terrier, came up to Andy's legs. Its tail wagged eagerly.

"Whiskers . . . *now* Whiskers—"

"No, it's fine."

Andy leaned forward and scratched behind the dog's ears, the dog tilting its head back, panting, its tail wagging even faster.

"You're a good dog, Whiskers," he said in a small voice. The dog's fur was coarse but Andy kept petting, the dog seemingly grinning as Andy worked behind its ears and then on its back.

"He's my best friend," the man said. He watched them, seeming wistful, before he reached into his pocket, taking out a tennis ball. "Want to give it a toss to him? My arm's not as good as it once was. Most things aren't." He chuckled.

"Oh. Okay. Sure." Andy took the ball from the man's wrinkled, shaking hand, and lifted it up high, Whiskers dropping to a sit, his gaze solely on the ball, focused, focused.

The old man unclasped the leash from Whiskers' collar.

Andy pulled his arm back and launched it some thirty feet, Whiskers bolting after it, grabbing it in his small mouth, and then bringing it back, eager for another.

"Okay, Whiskers, just one more," the man said. He joined his hands in his lap. "Go ahead, son."

Andy stood this time, throwing with all his might, Whiskers again darting after it, bouncing happily around the park, the nearby boy playing soccer with his father looking over and laughing with glee, Andy's arm slightly sore—but it all just feeling sort of right.

Whiskers came back with the ball, dropping it near Andy's feet.

The old man leaned over to pick it up but stopped. "Ooo, could you help me, son?"

"Sure."

Andy handed the ball to him. The man put it in his pocket and rose to his feet, grabbing the back of the bench for support. "Okay, Whiskers, what d'ya say we do another lap around the park? Then home. Papa's tired."

Andy reached down and petted Whiskers once more.

"Here, let me get that," Andy said, taking the leash from the old man and attaching it to Whiskers' collar.

"Say goodbye to your new friend," the old man said to the dog.

And then they walked away, the man's gait slow, while the dog's was buoyant, the two of them moving down the path together.

With them gone, Andy's aloneness became all the clearer. Really, he wouldn't have minded if the old man and "Whiskers" had stayed for a while. And going back to his parents' house was out of the question.

But then Shannon came to mind. There was no past with her—save for last night, which was hardly anything—and she was wholly unaware of the family drama. She was, basically, a clean slate in his life.

Andy took out his phone again and pressed the button for her number, his heartbeat kicking up in tempo and volume. He hardly knew this girl, but it was the possibility.

But then she answered.

"Hello?"

"Hey! It's Andy . . . the guy from last night."

"Oh hi."

"You sound a little better."

"Yep. I am feeling a *little* better. Not great but hanging in there."

"Good. Your room was warm or cool enough last night?"

"Ha yeah. You did a fine job with the thermostat."

"Good. Well listen . . . I'm pretty bored. You wanna . . . y'know, grab dinner or a drink or something?"

"Ah. Can't. It's the rehearsal and the rehearsal dinner tonight. I got to leave in a few minutes."

"Oh. Yeah. Right." Of course that would be tonight. He considered asking about tomorrow—but she'd have wedding stuff. Probably all day. Of course she wouldn't be free to gallivant around town with some random guy who had bugged her last night when she was sick—it all of a sudden seeming so clear, making him embarrassed that he had thought it would be any different. "Well . . . okay then. Okay. Have a good night."

He hung up before she could reply.

8

He rode the train the twenty-five minutes, and when he arrived, a sense of clarity came over him. The Kansas City Stoddard location was nice, sure, but the Chicago one, the original spot, standing before him now, was even nicer to look at, with its dark brick exterior, its original art deco sign from the 1930s, its revolving doors seemingly always moving with activity. He should've stayed here in the first place. After he got checked in, he'd call Taylor and let him know. It'd be a relief for both of them. Some people just weren't meant to spend a lot of time together. Candice, no matter how well-intentioned her desire for Andy to stay with them had been, would have to understand this.

Andy crossed the street and pushed through the revolving doors. The lobby was humming with people getting their room key cards, luggage waiting by their feet, and employees bouncing around, carrying bags and directing people to the elevators. An Asian couple was getting their picture taken in front of the small waterfall and fountain by the east side of the hotel. A family with young children was sprawled out on the leather couches in the center of the lobby, while the father looked over a map. In the corner a TV was showing a golf tournament.

When Andy got to the front of the line, the front desk clerk smiled. "Hi, welcome to the Stoddard. How may we help you today?" He looked around twenty-five, tall, and with short, light brown hair and hints of acne on his face. Andy didn't recognize him or any of the other employees.

"Yeah, hi, I'm Andy Canton."

"Okay, Mr. Canton," the employee said, furiously typing at his computer.

"No, no, I don't have a reservation. I work at the Kansas City location."

The employee stopped typing and looked up. "Oh cool."

"Yeah, I used to work here too."

"Oh yeah? That's pretty neat."

Andy was a little surprised the front desk clerk hadn't heard of him. Maybe he was just new.

"Yeah, I'm a manager," Andy said. "Well anyway, I'd like to get a room for tonight. Just a single. Any size bed is fine. I don't need anything special. Whatever's available. Sorry it's last minute and all."

"No problem at all," the employee said, turning back to his computer. "Let's see what we got here." He typed and clicked. "Hmm, we're actually pretty full—apparently there's a jewelry convention in town—so the cheapest available room we have is $349. A double bed. Tenth floor. Balcony. Fully-stocked mini-fridge. A separate shower and tub. Couch with additional pullout bed. Sound good? I'll just need a credit card."

"Well—no, I'm an employee, remember? I should get a free room, right? I mean, I've worked here for eight years. I know that's part of the perks."

"Hmm, I don't think so. I'm pretty new here, but—"

"Well, who's on duty? I mean, what manager? Let me just speak to them then." Andy looked around and finally saw the placard that said Jen Whitaker was on duty. Perfect. He and Jen went way back. "Oh Jen. Great. Can I talk to her?"

"Yeah, okay, I'll get her."

Andy heard a frustrated sigh from behind him in line. He glanced over his shoulder, the line extending a further five or six people back. The line for the other desk clerk looked similarly long. Why they only had two people working the front desk on a Friday evening was baffling—he'd mention it at the next work meeting, even though this wasn't his location.

Jen came out of the back room, clad in a solid black business suit and black heels.

"Well, Andy Canton. What a nice surprise," she said, coming up to him for a firm handshake, her hand feeling heavily-lotioned, her perfume lingering in the air.

Jen had been at the Stoddard for over ten years, previously working at high-end hotels in Cleveland and Denver. She had been a mentor, in a sense, to Andy, instilling in him the importance of hospitality, the art of it all—that it was more than just passing out key cards and listening to complaints with a consoling face. "So what are you doing in town?"

"Just visiting—well anyway, I was hoping to grab a room tonight, and this employee here"—Andy pointed, the employee frowning—"said it would cost me $349. Yeah, I can't believe that. Now, you know as well as I do, that employees can do stays of three consecutive days or less for free, but apparently he doesn't. Jen, you gotta train these people better." Andy smiled. The two of them had often playfully ribbed each other when he worked here.

"But not on Fridays or Saturdays, and today is Friday." Jen clasped her hands in a gesture of *case closed*.

A blank look came over Andy's face. "What? Since when was that stipulation made?"

"That's how it's always been. Did *you* not know that?" Her eyes narrowed. "I mean, it's a minor rule, but you need to know it. Maybe *you* weren't trained correctly. Surely not by me."

The nearby desk clerk stifled a smirk.

"Wow, okay, I hadn't heard that—are you sure that's always been the rule? I don't ever remember hearing that." He had, admittedly, never spent a night at the hotel, outside of that brief hook-up with a guest a few months ago, but he was almost a hundred-percent positive there were no blackout dates for employees staying the night, free of charge, assuming the hotel wasn't already full.

Jen closed her eyes and swallowed.

"Hunter," she said, motioning to the desk clerk, "I'll take care of this. Please help the next person in line. Folks, I'm sorry for your wait."

She flashed a smile at the next people in line, before placing her hand on Andy's shoulder and leading him to the side, some ten or twelve feet from the other people in line.

"To answer your question," she said, whispering, "*yes*, that's *always* been the rule."

"Oh. Well, come on, I think we can make an exception, right? I mean, I'm a manager—certainly, we can bend the rules a little bit."

"Um, no, I'm sorry, I won't do that." She shook her head. "I mean, you're a *night* manager at the *Kansas City* branch—you're hardly the CEO."

Andy flinched. He spotted a few guests looking over.

"But I've put in several years and—"

"Is something wrong, Andy?" Jen's eyes narrowed further. "Why'd you just . . . show up trying to get a room? I mean, it's none of my business, but you look a little, well, frazzled. You don't even have any baggage, it appears."

"Nothing's, uh—hey, but, come on, this is ridiculous—"

"It's the rules, Andy."

"Yeah, well, the rules are—the rules—they're fucking ridiculous."

"Hey, whoa." Jen looked around, her eyes appearing frantic as she checked the nearby guests for any reaction to the scene playing out in the corner. She pointed an index finger at Andy, and began speaking in a sort of shout-whisper. "You want me to call Dave and tell him about this? You want me to get security over here right now? I will not have you in my hotel acting like this."

"Oh come on—"

"Those are the rules. If you want a room, great. But you're going to pay the full rate. Otherwise, I'm going to have to ask you to leave."

The stern look stayed on her face.

Andy opened his mouth but was lost on what he could possibly say. He was . . . he was just asking for what he thought was only fair. What eight years of loyalty and hard work should've earned him, right?

He took a step back, suddenly aware what little stature he had at the hotel. He was not the rising star he had considered himself, someone with any real sort of "power." He was just a tiny cog in a large wheel.

He turned around and hurried out the front doors.

9

A ndy stood outside Taylor and Candice's front door, hesitating to knock. It felt like a failure returning here, but paying $349 for a room was ludicrous, and trying a different hotel seemed equally like a waste of money.

He finally knocked, but the door remained unanswered. He didn't even know if Candice and Taylor were here. They might still be at the house, going through things. He hadn't bothered to call ahead.

He knocked again and then heard a faint, distant voice say, "Just a minute."

Candice slowly opened the door.

"Andy, hey," she said.

She let him inside. Her eyes looked bloodshot, red.

They stared at each other.

She said, "I feel really bad about what happened earlier."

Andy peered around for Taylor, expecting to see him perched at his computer, working on schoolwork, or maybe in front of the TV, cycling through family videos.

"Where's Taylor?"

"He's still at the house. He'll be back in an hour or so. I took the train back. I had to . . . get out of there for a while."

"Everything okay?"

"That was really shitty what he did."

"Yeah, well." Andy shrugged.

Candice picked up her keys and purse. "I was actually about to go to the dog rescue. I haven't been all week and thought—yeah, just thought it might be nice for a couple hours. But—oh, you know, I can stay here."

"No, no, it's okay. I can just chill here. Maybe take a nap. Yeah, that'd probably be good."

"Well, let me at least make you a snack. I think there's some beer in the—"

"Really, it's okay."

"You sure?"

"My mother may be dead, but you don't need to mother me," Andy said, before seeing Candice's reaction. "Oh—no, sorry, I didn't mean that like—"

"It's okay. I guess I forget sometimes you're not your brother."

Andy pursed his lips, unsure what exactly she meant.

"Just . . . just don't be afraid to call if you need anything," Candice said, gripping the door handle. "It wouldn't be lame of you, you know."

Andy nodded, still somewhat confused, as she left out the door.

He stood in the entryway another moment before stepping over to the couch and dropping onto the deep cushions. He kicked off his shoes and then laid back on the pillow, hitting his head on a hardback book, an international relations book he then tossed on the floor.

He closed his eyes, but unsurprisingly, sleep did not come.

Changing positions did little either.

After a few minutes, he stood up and walked, sock-footed, around the apartment. In the refrigerator he saw hummus, ravioli, a container of strawberries, and other things. He was still pretty full from the Green Giant earlier—that thing was sitting in his stomach like a green brick—but he was a little thirsty, so he scanned the beverage options: cranberry juice, ginger ale, Coke Zero, and what looked to be a single beer. He reached for it but then pulled his hand back. It was the last beer after all; maybe he should leave that for them.

He closed the refrigerator door and continued pacing without any destination in mind. It was weird being in someone's home when they weren't there. The odd freedom that afforded you.

He stepped into Taylor and Candice's bedroom, only probably the second or third time he had ever set foot in there. The bed, with its large white comforter, was unmade—Candice had probably just jumped out of it a few minutes ago. She had looked sleepy, slightly disheveled, startled. The rest of the room, on closer inspection, seemed to have obvious dividing lines, the bed a neutral zone in the middle. Near Andy, things were mostly clean. The floor was free of anything save for one pair of women's flats, lined up side-by-side. On the nightstand were two neatly-stacked books, a candle, and a lamp, it all looking like a decoration you saw in homes for sale. The other side of the room, however, had a couple wrinkled shirts on the floor, a baseball glove, various computer cords, and several tall stacks of books against the wall by the window, where the spring sun was peeking through. Clearly Taylor's side.

Andy was aware his presence here—he by himself—was a violation of the inherent trust that bedrooms are off-limits to non-residents when the residents aren't home. Still, he found himself drawn to stay another moment. As he had learned today— even more so—he knew little of his parents' marriage outside of the face-value things he had witnessed as a kid, and even those were under question now after today's revelation.

Candice and Taylor's marriage was another thing he knew little about.

He headed for the dresser drawer and reached toward the handle, curious just what he'd find. Cracking it open a bit, he saw lacey black underwear, before he said out loud, "What the hell am I doing?" and closed the drawer, rattling a framed picture: Candice and Taylor at their wedding, smiling as they cut the cake.

The photo fell forward, landing facedown on top of the dresser.

Andy righted it and darted from the room, as if in danger of being caught. Upon entering the kitchen, his socked-feet slipped on the wood, and he tumbled to the floor, knocking the wind out of him.

He rolled onto his back and stared at the ceiling.

What was he doing? Doing here . . . doing now . . . *doing* in general?

Andy slowly stepped into Furry Friends, a couple blocks from Taylor and Candice's apartment.

"Well, hello there!" a woman sitting behind the front desk said. She clicked a couple more things on her computer and then stood up. "Interested in rescuing a dog or cat?"

Muffled barking came from the room behind her.

"Not exactly, but I'm—is Candice here? I'm her brother-in-law. Just thought maybe I could stop by and see the dogs?" He laughed at his random-sounding request, even if it was a place full of dogs. The dog at the park earlier . . . it had made him happy, less lonely.

"You're the brother of Candice's husband? Oh I'm so sorry," she said, her sunny demeanor slipping away. "I am so, so sorry. Please accept my deepest condolences." She pushed a curl out of her eyes.

"Oh. Yeah, thanks," Andy said.

The women looked back, consolingly.

"Candice?" Andy repeated.

"Oh! She's in the doggie clubhouse," the woman said. "Want me to get her?"

"The doggie clubhouse?"

"Haha. It's just one of the names for the room of dogs. Haha. Well here, just follow me. I'll take you back. Right this way."

They walked down a short hallway toward a door with a glass window that said "Doggie Clubhouse #1" in blue bubble letters.

"Okay," the woman said as she opened the door. "Here we are."

The room was lined with dog crates and pens, some of the dogs bouncing up and down, barking in enthusiasm, while others barely registered anyone coming in.

Howls and yips reverberated off the ceiling.

Behind one of the pen gates was Candice on her knees, scrubbing at the floor with a sponge.

"Candi, girl, you have a visitor?"

Candice peered up.

"Well, I'll leave you two," the woman said. "Hey, take a look at that Jack Russell near the back—think you'll like it. Just might change your mind about rescuing a friend." She winked.

A few dogs barked as she left the room.

"Hey. What . . . are you doing here?" Candice said.

Andy shrugged. "Tried to nap but—yeah, just thought it'd be fun to see the dogs."

"Well . . . here they are." She laughed tentatively.

Andy looked around, seeing dogs of all sizes, some in crates by themselves, while others were in pens with multiple dogs.

He took a step but then paused. He scratched at his nose. He swallowed.

"You ever," he said, struggling to make eye contact, "feel like you just need to 'get out'? But then you realize that you *always* feel that way?"

125

She took this in. "I'm not sure I understand what you're talking about."

"I don't mean, like, *permanently* get out, but just, y'know, that you're agitated or just always cranky or unhappy wherever you are or—maybe it's just this trip. God, it's been frustrating." He tried to laugh, but it came out like a muffled bark.

The dogs continued fidgeting in their crates or pens.

"I had to get out of the house earlier," Andy continued, "and then I went to the park but that was no good after a while, and then I went to the hotel I used to work at, and that, well, that wasn't happening, and then I came back to your place, even though I didn't want to see Taylor—I just . . . I just *fucking* hate that guy sometimes. I know he didn't mean to almost push me down the stairs—I'll give him that, but he just—how do you put up with him?" He scratched at his hair and then moved to behind his ear, tending to these phantom itches.

Candice swayed on her heels. "Well . . . I feel frustrated too. Just disappointed sometimes. Upset."

"Yeah—yeah, that's what I mean."

"And just angry. Just so angry. I mean . . . no, it's . . . fine. It's just a stressful—"

"No. Say it. Say you're angry," Andy said. "It's okay. You don't have to be the only mature one in this family."

"I'm angry!"

The dogs howled, the sound bouncing off the walls.

Andy and Candice laughed, short but there.

After a moment, Andy walked over to a nearby crate, seeing a black lab.

"Careful," Candice said. "They're not all friendly."

"It's okay. I don't think he'll push me down any stairs."

Andy put the back of his hand up to the cage door, the dog enthusiastically sniffing and licking his fingers.

Andy turned to Candice.

"When are you guys going to get another dog?"

Maybe he'd get one of his own when he got back to Kansas City—yeah, why not? Maybe that would ease his loneliness. Once you got through the housetraining period, assuming the dog wasn't nuts—well, it all just sounded pretty nice. Maybe pets were easier to deal with than humans.

But Candice stayed quiet, and then her eyelids began to flutter, and Andy realized she was crying.

"Oh hey," he said. "Sorry. I didn't—too soon? Sorry . . . Duffy was a great—"

"It's not that." It was the first time he had heard her voice like this—weak, thin, shaky.

Andy suddenly felt bad for coming here. He should've just stayed at the apartment, lying on the couch—or the *floor*—staring at the ceiling, just thinking. On his own. He didn't know showing up would upset her. He didn't—

"I'm leaving your brother," Candice said, still crying.

The dogs continued barking.

Andy dropped his hand from the cage door.

The black lab squirmed, rattling the metal.

"I can't do it anymore," Candice said. "I can't handle him. I can't stifle myself any longer. I'm sorry, but—"

"No, you're right. It's okay."

The black lab barked.

"We've been having problems for a while. A long while."

More dogs joined in the barking. The black lab shook the cage door.

"Let's get out of here," Andy said. "Come on."

Andy got them two beers, and brought them over to a table in the corner, where Candice was sitting. The bar was dark, dank, a dive bar a block from the apartment. Only a few people were inside, mostly men, alone. Bob Dylan was playing on the jukebox.

"Maybe we were stupid to get married so young," Candice said. She gripped the beer with both hands before taking a sip. Andy wasn't sure if he had ever seen her drink a beer before.

"No," Andy said. "It . . . it happens." He cut himself off, lost on what "advice" to give. What the fuck did he know about marriage anyway? About love?

"He didn't used to be so difficult. He used to be sweet. Maybe you didn't know that about your brother, but he can be very sweet, very kind. Protective. But—he hasn't in a long, long time." Candice consulted the table and then glanced back up at Andy. "And he's just directionless. You know this. A husband doesn't have to be a big shot to be somebody, but he has to do something, and I don't think he's ever going to do something." She looked into the distance, shaking her head. "You can only wait for the future to come for so long, for the thing you've supposedly been working toward to happen, before you say *enough*. My credit just sucks because of him. I make enough money for one person but not for two. . . . People have this inane idea that if you're a lawyer, you're rolling in money, but that's not true. . . . And I don't feel right using the money your parents left us in their will." She scratched at her eyelid. "He's not even doing that well in his classes. He had to do one course over again. He's a bit unrealistic if he thinks he could complete a Ph.D. His work's often late. The guy in charge of him at the internship is younger than him by a few years. That guy just has a B.A., but I think Taylor's just been obsessed with having a doctorate in *something* as if that would justify his aimlessness, his, obvious, indecisiveness about what to do with his life. Some of my friends have master's degrees or doctorates, but they seemed to have a plan; they're doing something. You know? I mean, I have a law degree! And I do in fact work as a lawyer! But Taylor . . . I just don't know what he'll do anymore."

All Andy could say was, "Oh."

"And I want kids," Candice said. She sniffled. "I do. I didn't when I was twenty-two. Neither did he, but . . . well, I'm a walking cliché, but something in me changed, something in me sees all my friends' and family's kids, and says I want one too, I want in on this facet of life . . . and something in him didn't, and I'm running out of time. I'm *running out of time.* That's maybe the biggest thing to me—I *want* kids. And he refuses."

"When are you going to . . . go through with this?"

"I don't know. I need all this stuff with your parents to pass. It's like everything went wrong all at once. You can't—oh, please don't tell him."

"I won't."

She kept staring at him.

"Seriously, you can trust me," Andy said.

"Okay."

A phone started ringing on the table, hers, startling the two of them. When had she set her phone there?

She cleared her throat and sat up straighter. "Hi . . . Andy and I, we just got a drink . . . yeah . . . sorry . . . okay, yeah, we'll, we'll head home now . . . yeah, we'll just be a minute."

She eyed Andy and then hung up the phone.

When they walked into the apartment, Taylor was standing by the kitchen table, where two pizza boxes were waiting.

"The pizza's getting cold," he said.

Candice said nothing.

Taylor straightened up. "Andrew, I'm . . . ," he began, his eyes falling to the table, "I'm really sorry for earlier. That was immature and wrong of me. I was upset, and reacted in an inappropriate way."

The apology seeming canned, his voice sounding almost robotic, devoid of genuine remorse, but Andy just shrugged, because just the fact he was getting an apology seemed like a miracle. "It's . . . fine."

Really, he felt somewhat sorry for his brother now, maybe more so than he ever had. Everyone was abandoning him. Andy hadn't known Taylor to be "alone" since he was twenty-one or so, when he met Candice and was always beaming about this brainy, beautiful girl, and even before then he had had their parents living close by, while Andy, by college, had begun, metaphorically at least, moving away from them all.

Candice set out plates and napkins, before sitting down at the end of the table opposite Taylor. Andy chose the perpendicular spot between them.

Without another word, they dug into the pizza, which had the kind of thick cheese and sauce that got momentarily lodged in your throat, spicy pepperoni swimming in grease, and garlic and peppery crust that tasted *so good* but caused you to pause for breath after each bite. It was Chicago deep-dish pizza, practically made to punish whoever ate it.

"That painting from the living room at my parents'?" Taylor said after a moment, looking toward Candice. "What do you think about putting it over here?" He pointed to the nearby wall. "I guess I could finally take the Ryne Sandberg poster down."

Candice finished swallowing, taking a few final, pointed bites before opening her mouth to speak. "Sure, that could look nice."

"We should get a new frame, though. The current one is chipped. Maybe next weekend?"

". . . Yeah, I could probably do that."

Andy just listened before taking another bite, remembering he had also had pizza yesterday.

Candice wiped her hands on her napkin. She glanced up, exchanging eye contact with Andy. She looked nervous, weary.

"Or do you have something going on next Saturday?" Taylor said. "I haven't looked at our calendar yet."

"I think I'm free. We'll see."

Andy wanted to bring up the note, not only to save Candice from discussing her and Taylor's future plans, but also to figure out what he and Taylor should actually do about it, but Andy knew it would only send Taylor into a rage, so why bother?

"I was thinking too," Taylor said, as he grabbed another slice from the box, "it's a little selfish of me to use all the inheritance for my tuition, and maybe I can get a graduate teaching assistantship when I start on my Ph.D. to offset some of the costs anyway, so. . . ." He smiled. "Maybe we could get a nicer, bigger place? Maybe a second bedroom we can use as an office or as a place for friends to stay when they're in town. Or family."

He set the pizza down and adjusted his glasses, still smiling.

Candice remained quiet. She glanced at Andy before looking up at Taylor. "Oh, we don't have to do that. This place is just fine."

Taylor's face fell. "I . . . I don't get it. I thought you'd be thrilled. You've thought this place was too small for years."

"No, no, that's really nice of you. I'm sorry. Yeah, that does sound like a really nice idea. I'm sorry . . . it's just been a busy, stressful day."

Her eyes darted to Andy for a second.

"Why do you keep looking at Andrew?" Taylor said, lowering his gaze.

"Oh, nothing."

"And why were you guys at a *bar* earlier?"

"We just got a drink, dude," Andy said.

"Yeah. You were at the house still," Candice said.

Taylor's face remained disbelieving. "Mmm-hmm." He drummed his fingers on the table. "You guys have been acting weird since you got back—is there something going on?"

Andy and Candice traded glances.

"There! You did it again," Taylor said.

"We just got a drink and talked," Andy said. "Just chilled out for a moment. It's been a stressful day for all of us."

Taylor continued staring. "Sometimes I wonder about you two."

"*Uh*, if you're implying your wife and I are having an affair, then, wow, you are so incredibly wrong."

"*Am* I wrong?"

"Taylor. Stop," Candice said, raising her voice. "Nothing is going on between me and Andy."

"Yeah," Andy said, and then it just seemed to slip out: "Your wife is not like mom—she wouldn't stab her family in the back."

Taylor slammed his fist down, hitting his plate and sending the new slice of pizza flying onto the rug. "Fuck!"

Candice jumped up and hurried to the kitchen to grab paper towels. Andy watched, baffled. Even after Taylor accused her of cheating on him, she was still willing to help him out.

"Stop!" Taylor said, getting to his feet. "I'll do it."

Candice said, "Here, let me—"

"No! I'll get it."

Candice surrendered a handful of paper towels to Taylor who took them to the rug and got down on his knees. He began scrubbing, gritting his teeth, while Candice remained in the kitchen, blankly sipping a glass of water.

Andy sat there, watching his brother labor over the mess, but his gaze soon blurred as his mind wandered . . . what a shitty thing to say . . . *their mom had "backstabbed" their family.* . . . Andy, he loved her. He didn't personally feel backstabbed . . . just confused. Just *let down* in some way. And even if she had done what the note implied . . . she was his mother. She had been a good mother. A good person. It didn't excuse what she did . . . but . . . well. . . . And it was just amazing how seemingly tiny choices could have such ramifications—in this case, his inane insistence on extracting the, what, dollar and thirty cents of spare change from his mom's piggy bank. Why had that seemed so fucking important? If he hadn't acted like a kid eagerly rifling through his parents' stuff, the shittiness of today wouldn't have happened. He could've happily lived a lie the rest of his life—that his biological parents were Walter and Helen Canton. Many people lived lies, and turned out perfectly fine.

Eventually the three of them moved to their own separate places in the apartment that couldn't be more than five-hundred or six-hundred square feet. They were away yet still in close proximity to each other. Taylor went to the bedroom, slamming the door behind him, while Candice sat at the kitchen table, doing something on her laptop, the rug under her feet dotted with, perhaps, permanent hints of a pizza stain. On the couch, Andy stared at his still-unfinished eulogy, his mind almost as blank as the page. He opened "Eulogy Ideas.docx," but it did little to get ideas flowing. What was he going to do anyway, share a bunch of silly anecdotes about how his parents liked sports, how they had favorite bands, how his mom liked to laugh—what was so interesting about that? And certainly the news of his mom's actions only left him more confused as to what to say.

He leaned his head back. It was only 9:00, but he could see falling asleep right now, the pizza still sitting heavily in his stomach, like an anchor weighing him down, down, down.

He closed his eyes.

In two days, he'd head home. Back to life in Kansas City. Back to a routine that was sometimes boring, yeah, but not *this*.

He had the feeling that there was so much he needed to do when he got back, but when he tried to think of just what that was he drew a blank.

He was both very busy and had all the time in the world.

He was beginning to warm more to the idea of just surrendering to sleep, when his phone started buzzing in his pocket.

He opened his eyes, momentarily disoriented—wait, had he actually fallen asleep?—and then pulled out his phone to see a text from Shannon.

This rehearsal dinner is the worst! I knew it. Want to hang out?

He grinned. The answer was of course yes—not just to get out of this apartment but to be with her—yet he glanced back at his computer, specifically the blinking cursor on the screen, taunting him. The funeral was tomorrow morning, his eulogy due to be read in thirteen or fourteen hours. But who was he kidding, thinking he could give some great speech? The idea of speaking in front of people terrified him. People who weren't scared of that were crazy or at least full of themselves.

Or maybe he was just looking for a "valid" reason to give Taylor and Candice for why he, Andy, shouldn't give a speech too.

He tapped his fingers on his phone, texting back: *yeah thatd be cool, lets.*

10

When Andy saw Shannon standing in front of the Console, a barcade in Wicker Park that he had recommended, he could feel himself already getting attached. Even more so.

She was pretty, she was here, she was an opportunity.

He knew it was ridiculous to put so much stock in a girl he had known maybe twenty-four hours, but it was nice to spend time with someone with no ties whatsoever to his family, his family that was seemingly falling apart.

"Hey," he said.

Her head shot up from her phone, and she smiled and considered him a second before they hugged. When they separated, she slunk back, looking almost embarrassed. "What would you say about going somewhere else?"

"Oh. You don't want to go here anymore? It's—"

"I was just thinking, you know, I've never seen the lake before?"

"Oh. It's nice, but it's pretty touristy, but—"

"So, I don't really want to go into it, but there's someone here I just don't really want to see. . . ."

"Oh. Okay. Yeah. Sure."

"It's not that interesting anyway—why I don't want to see them."

Them. She didn't even want to identify the gender.

"Okay. Okay. That's fine," Andy said, his level of excitement deflating.

What was going on?

"Here, I'll get a Sher, and we'll head over there," she said. "Sound good?"

"Sure."

Andy stood by while she pulled up the ride-sharing app on her phone.

When a car rolled up a few minutes later, a black Toyota, sound blasting from inside, they got in the back.

"What's up?" the guy yelled from the driver's seat. He lowered the hip-hop coming from the stereo, but it remained loud. He tapped the Bluetooth on his right ear. On the dashboard were numerous cords. Attached to the front air vents was a plastic arm holding an iPhone with GoogleMaps on the screen. A twenty-ounce bottle of Mountain Dew: Code Red stood in the cup holder, half-drunk.

"We're going to Navy Pier," Andy yelled, unsure exactly what their plan was. "Just anywhere around there will be fine."

The guy pulled out another cell phone and texted a few things, before placing it on his right leg.

"All right, let's do this," the guy said and bumped his fists together.

Without appearing to look, he pulled into traffic.

Andy sat back and glanced at Shannon.

"It's just someone from my past," she said, leaning toward him. "Sorry, I'm just—yeah, I'm just being emotional, ha. It was not an ex or anyone, but just . . . someone I didn't want to see. You probably have some of those."

"Hmm. Yeah, maybe."

"I guess I'm just a little fragile at the moment—sorry."

"Something happen at the rehearsal dinner?"

The car jerked to the side. Shannon and Andy reached their hands out, grabbing the back of the front seats.

Andy peered around and realized the guy had just changed lanes.

"Friday night traffic, a *bitch*," the guy said. He texted something using the cell phone on his leg. He gunned the engine and then changed lanes again.

Andy peaked over the guy's shoulder and saw the speedometer. He was going probably fifteen over the speed limit. Not exactly fast, but—

Shannon leaned toward Andy. "The rehearsal dinner was fine, but I guess . . . just weddings, ha, *got me down*," she said, saying the last part in a different voice.

"Weddings can be rough when you're single."

"It's like all my Facebook is these days—just photos and photos of engagement rings."

"The huge close-ups of the ring."

"Yes! It's so annoying. I don't need to see fourteen different angles of the same ring! Rebecca did that. And posted the whole proposal story."

"Yeah. I've never even proposed to anyone, but I feel this pressure that if I would, I have to do some elaborate thing," Andy said, grinning. "Like, I have to enlist the entire Chicago Bears to help me. And all of it *has* to be captured on video and posted online."

"Just being asked—*that* should be the nice thing," she said. "I'd just like to be asked."

Andy looked over.

She kept talking, staring straight ahead, but her voice trailed off.

"You okay?" he said.

"I'm fine."

The guy changed lanes again, throwing Andy and Shannon around in their seats.

Andy glared at the back of the guy's head, as if hoping to transmit his annoyance without the guy seeing or hearing it.

"Let's make a deal," Shannon said, turning to Andy. "Whatever happens, let's never get lame or predictable or cliché."

"Ha. Okay," Andy said.

She reached out, and the two of them grasped hands in the configuration of people making a pact.

"But I'm sure we're just as lame as everybody else," Andy said, smirking.

"Come on." She appeared almost desperate.

"Okay. Sure. Consider it a deal."

"Good."

Their clasped hands bopped up and down, as if banging a gavel to signal the start of something.

Shannon laughed, embarrassed, and they traded glances, and Andy's hands fell to her legs and stayed there, and it seemed like the perfect time to lean forward and—

"Oh fuck!" the driver said.

The car jerked and slammed to a stop, a one-two punch as it banged into a car in front of them, throwing Shannon and Andy's bodies, that had been facing each other, into the back of the seats in front of them, Shannon's forehead smacking Andy's.

"Fuck!" the guy said again, their car now at a dead stop.

Andy looked around, confused, his neck aching, Shannon similarly wincing as she rubbed at her shoulder.

"Owww," she said.

"What just happened?" Andy said, removing his seatbelt.

"The—the car in front of me was just stopped. I mean, I couldn't have—"

"You fucking weren't paying attention," Andy said.

Music continued pumping from the stereo.

"No, they were stopped."

"Cause it's a stoplight!"

Andy helped Shannon remove her seatbelt. "You okay?"

"I think so."

"Fuck! Fuck!" the guy continued yelling. He punched his steering wheel.

Andy slowly got out of the car, which was some twenty feet from the stoplight at Diversion and Hendricks. The cars around them remained stopped, pedestrians and drivers hurrying over on foot, while

141

some cars zoomed around them, zipping through the intersection.

There seemed to be some loud talking in the background. People calling out. Questions.

There didn't appear to be serious damage but some. To both cars.

Andy helped Shannon out of her seat. She looked fine but startled. Then he opened the front door, where the guy looked back at him, scared. A line of blood came from his lip.

"Are you okay?" Andy said. "Do you have a first aid kit or—"

"I . . . it just happened," the guy said, still in a daze.

He slowly got out of the car, his cell phone falling off his lap and onto the street. He bent over and grabbed it. "*Owwww.*"

The driver from the car in front of them, a woman in her mid-forties, hurried back to them, alarmed, already on her phone, calling somebody. The back of her car was pretty smashed, but it looked fixable.

"Is everyone okay? What happened? Are you all right?"

"You didn't have your lights on or something. I didn't see you," the Sher driver said.

She looked back, puzzled. "My lights were on. See." She pointed at the back of her car at one of the rear lights broken and dangling but still turned on.

"You could've just turned those on before you got out of your car," the guy said.

"What?" the woman said.

"You were fucking texting," Andy said to the driver of his car. "You weren't paying attention."

"That's not true! I—"

"Just be honest."

"Well, I—It's not like—"

"Yeah, that's what I thought. Well, maybe if you had been paying attention and not trying to run a mobile command unit or whatever you're doing in your car, then this wouldn't have happened. Your car wouldn't be fucked up, and this woman's car wouldn't be either, and we all wouldn't be rubbing at our necks cause they hurt."

Sirens and red lights swirled behind them as a cop car arrived at the scene.

"You're an asshole. You are a complete asshole," Andy said, the anger growing inside him, an anger he didn't know he possessed. It was one thing to yell at your family—growing up practically prepared you to—but unleashing venom on a stranger. . . . "You know what, man? You want to hear something? My parents died in a car accident, what, four days ago. *Four* days ago. You could've killed someone. You're an *asshole*. Fuck you, man. Fuck you."

People continued to stand there, watching. A small crowd had formed. The woman lowered the phone from her ear. Shannon remained quiet. The driver from their car flinched but looked back at them, startled, lost on how to respond.

The nearby cop closed the door on his car and stepped over, holding onto his belt.

"You're an *asshole*," Andy said one more time, jabbing his index finger in the air.

After various paperwork was filled out and statements given, and they were told they could go, Andy and Shannon, who hadn't said anything to each other in ten minutes, stood on the sidewalk.

"Well, you still want to go to Navy Pier? Ha."

"I think maybe I should just go back to the hotel," Shannon said.

"I'm sorry, I shouldn't have blown up like—"

"Your parents died a few days ago?"

"Oh. Yeah. They did. That's, that's why I'm in town."

"I'm so sorry," she said. "And here I was, whining about my stupid 'problems.' "

"No, that's totally fine."

"No, it's not."

"I guess I should've told you, but it just—I don't know, I just felt weird talking about it."

"Well, I know this is a weird thing to say to someone I just met, but, don't hesitate to talk about it. Or anything. I don't mind. Maybe that'll help."

"Thanks."

"You want to walk me home? I don't think we're that far from my hotel."

Andy brightened. "Sure. Okay."

They began moving away from the scene of tow trucks and flashing cop car lights and another cop directing traffic, and Shannon reached out and rubbed Andy's back, and he smiled and felt okay.

"And my sister and I just didn't talk for a long time. A really long time," Shannon said. Andy saw the

Premiere Hotel in the distance. It was getting too close. "And our younger brother seemed to take my side more, but I just felt terrible, really. We both just had to say sorry and look past it."

"You guys sound way more mature than Taylor and I."

"We're still not perfect."

"I think I've wasted a lot of time trying to be perfect," Andy said, "when I couldn't be more far from perfect."

"I think I've wasted a lot of time in general. We all do."

"You ever think about all the stuff you worried about or cared about and how later, when you look back on it, it was all meaningless, like why were you so concerned about it at one time?"

"Well . . . I don't think it's meaningless just cause those things no longer worry you. They're still very real."

The sounds of the city at night, a dull hum of traffic and people, surrounded them.

God, he liked talking to her.

He intentionally slowed his gait to prolong this last two hundred feet before they'd arrive at the sliding front doors of the Premiere.

But then they were there. Once again a person was smoking within twenty feet of the doors, which opened up as a couple walked out, laughing about something, the woman gripping the man's arm. A car pulled out of the overhang. Cigarette butts lay in the bed of a nearby plant.

Shannon stopped and turned to Andy.

"So I think we should say goodnight here. Sorry if you were hoping to . . . well. . . ."

"Oh. That's okay."

They stood there, idling, like high schoolers on a first date, rocking back and forth on their heels. Andy didn't know what had soured their night—the unnamed person she had run into? The relatively minor, though annoying, car accident? . . . But you would think two people who had just been through a car accident—if it wasn't one of their faults, if they were alive and okay—might be suddenly closer.

The revelation about his parents?

Had his parents had a moment before they died where they suddenly felt closer? Had they known they were both about to die?

And he had, of course, hoped he'd be invited into her room.

So much of life was hoping to be invited into somewhere.

Finally Andy pulled her close, kissing her, gripping her waist. She leaned into him, her pelvis making contact with his, her lips soft, chapped.

When they stopped, Andy said, "You sure I can't come up for a bit? We don't have to do anything. I'm not trying to pressure you into anything."

"Listen," she said, looking down and then back up at him. "I just got out of a long relationship. Like . . . seven *years* long."

"*Seven* years. Wow. How long ago?"

"Two weeks."

Andy's eyebrows darted up. "Wow. Well . . . that's okay, but look, you can't scare me off that easily."

She laughed, pushing the hair out of her eyes.

Andy continued, "Tomorrow's my last night in town. Want to do something? You know, just hang out, have fun."

"Tomorrow's the wedding."

"Oh right. Well, I guess—"

"You want to go?" she said suddenly. "I mean, I think they'd be cool if I bring someone. A lot of people aren't going to be there, because it's out of town for a lot of the guests. Yeah, you should come. I'll make sure it's okay with Rebecca, but she won't care. She had assumed I was bringing my boyfriend anyway."

Andy smiled. "Yeah, I'd like that."

"Good."

She gave one more smile, before turning to step through the sliding doors and into the hotel, Andy grinning as he began the walk to Taylor and Candice's place.

11

In the slow footsteps to the large front doors of Grace United Methodist Church, a sort of family reunion began forming, as aunts, uncles, cousins, grandparents, and other people greeted each other, looking extra remorseful at Taylor and Andy. Andy returned the solemn smiles, but part of him, in all honesty, felt light, happy, okay. He had woken up still thinking about Shannon and experiencing an enthusiasm for someone he hadn't had in a couple years. It felt like a crime against humanity to actually be in a decent mood at a funeral, no less one for your own parents. But he was.

His only duty now was to get through the rest of the day until he could see her tonight.

When they walked into the sanctuary, Andy saw an altar near the front with two urns among several framed photographs and bouquets of flowers. He was surprised—his parents had been cremated? For some reason he had expected to see two caskets side-by-side, closed hopefully—caskets he and Taylor and the other able-bodied men would be expected to carry out, struggling under the weight of wooden boxes and what was inside them.

Taylor led them to the front row on the right side. Ominous organ music was being played by a middle-aged bald man in the corner.

"Let's sit farther back," Andy said.

"We're the family," Taylor said. "We sit in the front row."

"Oh."

The idea of sitting in the front row felt extra nerve-wracking, like everyone would be glancing their way—the poor Canton twins—to see who cried, who remained stoic.

Andy sat down on the hard pew bench. In front of him were a Bible, hymnal, and note cards inviting people to sign in and leave their personal information. He left those alone.

"You got your speech?" Taylor said, pulling his out of his pocket. He had been quiet all morning, perhaps glum over the funeral or still upset about last night. Andy didn't know nor ask.

The whole car ride had been mostly silent, the three of them in their own worlds.

Taylor opened the pages, revealing his speech was double-spaced, twelve-point Times New Roman font, and with some lines crossed out by pen, as if he had been up late, laboring over it.

Shit.

"I was thinking," Andy said, "what if just you give a speech? Yours would be better than mine anyway."

"You didn't write anything, did you?"

"I. . . ."

"If you don't feel comfortable," Candice said, "you don't have to speak."

Taylor frowned. "You said you would—"

"I'll say something," Andy said. "Yeah. I will."

Taylor sighed.

Andy turned to gaze at the organist, who was wearing a rumpled black suit and had a noticeable ring of sweat on the top of his head like a halo. He rocked forward and backward, as his feet pressed different pedals while he played on two rows of keys, the organ's large brass tubes ringing with the funeral music.

Was this the consolation job pianists took when their Billy Joel rock star dreams didn't pan out?

And just why did funerals need a soundtrack?

Andy looked down at his clasped hands, his white knuckles. He turned to the altar and the urns. He recognized the family portrait from Taylor's mantle, a smaller version, placed as a sort of centerpiece between the two urns, as if he and Taylor had died as well—or as if the photo were saying, "you two are next."

Andy gazed around the church. He hadn't been here in probably ten years. Who had set up this service? Taylor, most likely. And how did you even set up a funeral? Did the minister get paid? Did he enjoy doing things like this, or was he annoyed he was missing sports or something else on his Saturday morning? How did any of it work? And why did he, Andy, have so many stupid, meaningless questions this morning when he should be focusing on who was in those urns? There were times he felt like a card-carrying adult, and other times like a total child, just not knowing how anything worked, how things were done. Maybe it was like how some of his friends would start talking about their mortgages or the pros and cons of epidurals or why it was important to aerate your lawn, and his eyes would glaze over due to the unfamiliar terms, their lives sounding like something he'd never know.

And what does "refinancing" actually mean?

Andy's eyes continued traveling around the sanctuary. A couple dozen more people had shown up, some family members, some co-workers of his dad probably, and some others. It was nice of them to come out.

The minister, a tall, gaunt man, maybe seventy, rose from his chair at the front, his chair resembling some sort of gilded throne from medieval times, and moved to the center of the stage.

The guests soon quieted down.

The organ music stopped abruptly.

"Good morning. I welcome everyone to Grace United Methodist Church. Welcome. I wish it were on a higher note. I wish we weren't here to mourn the passing of two parents"—he looked down at Taylor and Andy, a glint in his eyes. Andy had never even seen this guy before, but Taylor must've met him—"aunts, uncles, cousins, brothers and sisters, two children of God. But we must remember in the bigger picture of things it is not a sad day, as Walter and Helen are now with their maker, their eternal father."

He gave a consoling smile to the room.

Andy heard Taylor sniffle, his eyes looking wet already, his head hung slightly down. Taylor reached over and grabbed Candice's hand, Candice flinching at first.

"Death is not easy. We know that the death of Jesus was anything but easy. But still we each must experience death, but we can do so knowing there is hope. . . ."

Andy began zoning out, while Taylor continued tearing up, occasionally releasing his grasp of Candice's hand to wipe a tear from his eye, before returning the now wet hand to hers. In between glancing at the minister who was sharing thoughts on Walter and Helen both having died relatively young—or wait, was he talking about some sort of mission trip they all did once?—Andy again peered around the church, noticing the architecture, the layout, all things he had never really considered before, including the stained-glass windows, which though beautiful, he couldn't help but think the money used for them could've—and maybe should've—been given to charity instead.

"Walter and Helen were devoted members of Grace United," the minister continued. "Their generosity and service will be missed."

But, come on—why couldn't he feel the emotion he was supposed to feel now? Why was he instead concerning himself with how the church's money was allocated or wondering just who set up the funeral? Who cared?

It was his parents in those urns.

But when he looked at them, all he saw were decorative vases.

How could his parents be in those tiny vases?

Andy snapped to attention when the minister started singing without musical accompaniment, the minister gesturing with his opened palms in a submissive pose toward heaven. The reason for this a cappella performance was lost on Andy. It seemed strange, out of place, even if it was most likely a hymn.

"In your arms . . . in your arms at last. . . ."

When the minister finished, he called Taylor to the front.

Taylor rose to his feet, taking a deep breath before stepping up to the stage.

He pulled a bottled water out of his pocket— where had that come from?—along with his notes.

"Hi," Taylor said from the podium, before stepping back to clear his throat. He sighed loudly. He lifted up his glasses and wiped at his eyes. "Phew, this will be difficult. Okay." He took another step back, exhaling, before grasping the podium with both hands. "As all of you know, and Pastor Donnelly said so well, my parents Walter and Helen Canton were beautiful people. They did what was right, they treated others with respect, they raised my brother and me in a house of love. They taught me what love is. I hope my marriage with my wife, Candice, is even half as good as theirs." He looked at Candice, smiling.

Taylor glanced down at his notes and continued, "I've felt lost since I heard the news. Lost for the right words. Lost for the right emotions. Lost in my own life, but I'm thankful I still have my wife, my brother, and other family members to help me when I've needed it. That's what I think we should all remember. That while we may lose people, we never truly lose them, and in their place other people can remind us how not alone we really are. So I'm thankful for that."

Taylor continued from there, pausing occasionally to wipe at his eyes or catch his breath or take a sip from his bottled water, the bottle making a crinkling sound every time he squeezed it, the plastic screech ringing out in the large sanctuary. Andy watched with subtle awe. Taylor was a very good public speaker, even if what he said sounded over-dramatic and at times a rather liberal stretch of the truth. Candice, meanwhile, wiped sporadically at her eyes with a scrunched-up tissue. Andy's eyes remained dry.

"So now," Taylor said, putting his notes in his pocket, "I'll hand things over to my brother, Andrew. Andrew?"

Andy jerked to attention from his dazed stare. Taylor came down the steps toward Candice who hugged him before they sat down. Seemingly echoing through the room were the sounds of sniffling and blowing noses, the equivalent of applause for funeral speeches. Andy staggered to his feet. For basically the first time on the trip, he didn't feel sick from food or drink, but he still felt shaky, and a tingling took over his body, as he climbed up the three steps to the podium. He was thankful there was this physical object to hold him upright, to act as an anchor, to be a slight barrier between him and the crowd of people staring at him, all with morose expressions, their faces making him shake even more. How did people do this? How did the minister do this every week?

"Um, thanks, Taylor, for those . . . remarks." Andy cleared his throat. "I'm admittedly not as good a speaker as my brother. I guess he got the good speaking skills, and I got . . . ha . . . the good looks." He paused for laughter, but the room stayed silent. His heart was pounding in his chest, like it was trying to climb out of his throat, his whole body being put through a rigorous stress test. If he were older he would've thought he was having a heart attack. He coughed a couple times into his sleeve. "Um . . . I don't have much to say—I mean, I think Taylor covered it, uh, you know, he covered it pretty well." Andy looked up at the mourners, sweat forming on his forehead and every other place sweat could suddenly start. He made eye contact with Taylor who stared back with indignation.

A few pews away a baby began crying, the mother—Andy and Taylor's cousin Irene—clutching the baby to her shoulder and quickly hurrying out of the sanctuary, causing a murmur in the pews.

"But yeah, I'm sad they're gone. It was a terrible thing. I hadn't talked to them in a while. I was, you know, very busy in Kansas City." Andy felt himself reeling, his stomach churning. He sounded like a true asshole, his speech perhaps validating why people needed religion to straighten themselves out, to make them not be so selfish. "But I hope they were happy. Together. That's, yeah, that's pretty cool." He rocked slightly forward, suddenly dizzy, catching himself. Was he about to faint? He grabbed onto the podium for balance. "I mean, that's not cool they—*passed*, but I hope they were happy together until that very last moment. Together, I mean. And—" He gazed out at the crowd again, but this time he saw near the back of the room a man with a mustache and dark brown hair with hints of gray in it, a man Andy immediately recognized as Skip Potter, sitting alone, his eyes downturned in the look of sadness.

Oh. . . .

Skip Potter.

Oh—

Andy paused and felt his body rock some more. He grabbed the podium even tighter and tried to look away from the man.

"Oh boy . . . phew. . . ." He jerked, clenching his eyes shut. "I'm sorry, I'm not—oh. *Ohhh.*" His voice cracked. He grabbed his mouth with both hands and coughed twice, a quick *ungh-ungh* that filled his mouth with his breakfast, the wet, sticky mess seeping past his pale fingers.

A gasp arose from the crowd.

The minister hurried over with a box of tissues.

Andy re-swallowed the contents in his mouth, wincing as it returned to where it had been, and accepted a tissue from the minister, wiping at his mouth, his head down, his eyes clenched shut.

"That's okay, Andrew. That's okay," the minister said, embracing him and gently patting him on the back.

Taylor jumped to his feet, taking Andy from the minister's grasp, as if Andy were a kid needing to be corralled by his father. He led Andy to his seat, Andy feeling even more confused but mostly embarrassed. What, what—

The minister resumed talking, again gesturing animatedly with his hands, again holding his palms high and upturned. It took everything in Andy not to turn around now and stare into the eyes of Skip Potter, despite his head still feeling woozy and heavy, or to jump up and grab him by the lapels and shake him until he gave an honest answer about whether there was ever anything between Skip and Andy's mom.

But then all of a sudden, the organ started playing and people stood up, beginning to mill around, and Andy again snapped to attention, seeing several family members hugging, the minister walking among them, shaking hands and sharing embraces.

Soon Andy found himself in the large, sweaty arms of his Uncle Lyle.

"Andrew, I feel so terrible," Lyle said in his husky southern drawl. He had grown up in Chicago with his brother, Andy's dad, but after serving in the army and relocating to Mississippi, he had picked up a decidedly Southern accent, which had somehow not similarly developed in his daughter Irene or his wife—*third* wife—Farah, both of whom Andy assumed were with Irene's baby out in the hall. "It's a shame, *it* is a shame. Lord knows I'll miss him and your mom. We didn't always see eye-to-eye, your father and I, and now I regret that more than anything."

"I'll miss them too," Andy said, wishing he could see over his uncle's hulking shoulders. Suddenly there seemed nothing more important than finding Skip and talking to him.

Lyle held Andy at arm's length. "I know you and I don't talk much either—we all get caught up in our own lives—but I want you to know I am here for you. *For you.*" He shook Andy, as if really trying to send this message home. "*And* Taylor. Both y'all."

"Thanks, Uncle Lyle."

Lyle pulled him into one more hug, the most physical contact the two of them had ever had outside of vice-like handshakes so strong they had almost brought Andy to his knees.

"I just had no idea he was depressed," Lyle said, shaking his head with guilt. "I guess we didn't speak enough."

"He was . . . depressed?"

"Yeah, your father. He was on new meds, Zoloft or something, you know, those commercials where people are always walking on beaches aimlessly. If I lived near the beach, I certainly wouldn't be depressed. But anyway, those meds can mess with you, I've heard. I wouldn't touch them myself."

Andy took this in, it hitting him hard. What had his father been depressed about? What emotions his father had felt, Andy hadn't ever really known. He had never seen his father's "backstage," his "behind the scenes." He had only seen the calm, collected version of his dad, the patriarch of the Canton family, high IQ, hard-worker, generally a quiet man, but with a strong sense of humor.

Depressed?

Since when?

Oh.

He had always been like Andy in a way, not one to really open up to family about his feelings and what was going on.

"They say don't operate heavy machinery, or what have you, until you've figured out how it affects you," Lyle continued. "But I think your father was just so sedated, or what have you, that he just fell asleep. We put Henry on them, a different pill, once, and it made him so sleepy all the time, just falling asleep in class and so on. It only made things worse."

Lyle gave Andy's shoulder one more intense squeeze, and then walked away.

Andy stared at the slightly stained green carpet before looking up and seeing his grandfather, his mom's father, slowly ambling his way, the tennis ball-footed walker keeping him on two feet.

"Hi, Grandpa," Andy said.

His grandfather, who as far as Andy knew was not visually impaired, looked almost startled by a voice near him. "Hi there."

"I'm . . . sorry for your loss," Andy said.

What was he supposed to say to his grandfather who had just seen his daughter in an urn?

"Mmm-hmm," his grandfather nodded and then kept moving on past him.

Andy stood there a moment before hurrying down the aisle to find Skip, but he wasn't still in his seat. He spun around and scanned the entire crowd, but he couldn't see him. He had to be here. He had to. He wouldn't have just jetted like that.

But still, Andy couldn't find him. He couldn't find him anywhere.

12

Andy sat in the back of Taylor's car as Taylor drove the three of them to Irene's house, where she was hosting a light lunch and reception.

"I can't believe you couldn't muster the energy to write a speech for our parents' funeral," Taylor said, glaring at Andy in the rearview mirror. "That is so selfish."

Andy sighed, more annoyed at himself than at Taylor's complaining. "I started one but . . . yeah, I'm sorry." He fidgeted in his seat. He glanced out the window. Traffic was busy. Pedestrians lined the sidewalks. It looked cold. "I'm not sure why it was necessary for both of us to give speeches anyway."

Taylor scoffed. "I think it's the *least* you could've done."

". . . Yeah."

After a moment, Andy said, "Did you know Dad was depressed?" He leaned his head back on the headrest, the car gently rocking beneath him.

"What makes you think he was 'depressed'?" He said "depressed," like it was a foreign word.

"Uncle Lyle said so. He said Dad was taking Zoloft or whatever, and that that may have made him so sleepy that that's why he fell asleep at the wheel."

Taylor scoffed again. "That's just Lyle making up things. Come on. He was probably drunk when he said it. You know that."

"He didn't seem drunk."

"He seemed fine to me," Candice added.

"What are you doing, Andrew?" Taylor said, slapping his hand on the steering wheel. He looked again in the rearview mirror, a parent eying his disobedient child. "I know I keep saying this, but it *continues* to happen: it's like you're trying to stir up trouble this weekend." He squeezed the steering wheel with both hands. "Our mom was an adulterer, our father was depressed and on medication. What next?"

Andy sat back, shaking his head. There was more he could say . . . that Skip Potter had been at the funeral, for one, but with Taylor, it was just pointless.

He just needed to get through the rest of the day. Just get *through*.

Taylor parked the car a few houses down from Irene's, and the three of them walked in silence to the front door. On the front step next to a potted plant was a large stone that said, in a cursive script, *The Gregory's*—the incorrect apostrophe something Andy had long wanted to correct them on but hadn't bothered, this apostrophe extra baffling considering Irene's husband Grant was a journalist.

After Taylor knocked on the screen door, Grant, in shiny black dress pants and a shiny gray shirt with a black tie hanging from his neck, came to the door, his two golden retrievers trailing behind him, bouncing up and down. With one hand, he inched open the door, while trying to block the dogs from jetting outside.

"Hey guys," Grant said, fretting. "Come on, Tropper, Percy." He held the two golden retrievers by the collar as they lunged toward Taylor, Andy, and Candice.

Once the three of them were inside, with the screen door closed behind them, Grant let go of the dogs, sending them into a further frenzy, as they jumped up and down at the new guests.

"Down! Down!" Grant said, though the dogs didn't abide. He reached out to grab them, but their frantic movements eluded his large hands. "Ah. Sorry, guys. Irene? *Irene!?*" He chuckled. "Well, they must smell Duffy on you."

"Duffy died—oh—*ah*—eee—a month ago," Taylor said, squirming and cowering under Percy's lunging.

"Oh, that's right. Sorry. We sent you a card, didn't we?" Grant stood there with his arms folded, having apparently given up on corralling the dogs.

"Hey guys, over here. Come on," Candice said, patting her knees. She bent down. The dogs rushed over, furiously licking and nudging her face. She giggled.

"Irene!?" Grant yelled. "*Irene!*"

Irene came into the foyer, bouncing the baby on her hip. "What is it? Oh, Tropper, Percy. Outta here! Come on! Out! *Now*!"

The dogs bounded into the living room, where several family members were seated.

"Oh honey, that's a beautiful dress," Irene said, bouncing the baby. She walked over to Candice, swatting at her dress to get the loose dog hair off. Andy looked down at his own clothes, seeing hair and paw prints everywhere. He wiped at his pants. He'd have to get this all off before the wedding tonight.

"Oh, that's okay," Candice said. "Really—yeah. That's fine."

From the living room came, "*Ooof*! Hey fellas! No, no, don't eat—aw."

"Oh sheesh. Well, come on in, everyone," Irene said, hurrying into the living room. "Outside! Outside!" she yelled, the dogs' collars and tags jingling as she opened the back door, the two of them fighting to be the first one out.

Still in the foyer with the three of them, Grant fingered the large, no-doubt expensive, gold watch on his left arm, before scratching the back of his head. "Sorry about that. Ha. Is your dress okay, Candi?"

"Yeah, it's fine."

"Good. Well, like the Mrs. said. Come in, come in." Anything Grant said, in his booming baritone voice, sounded like an important message, like the pre-recorded voice giving instructions on the train or at the airport. That plus the 5:00 shadow seemingly forever on his face and his dark black hair with hints of gray around his temples made him seem near fifty, even though he was late thirties at most. He was TV handsome, which suited him well for his job as a nightly anchor on the local NBC affiliate. Because of this job, the other family members frequently treated him like a celebrity. Andy too had been momentarily star-struck when he met Grant eight or nine years ago at a Christmas Eve dinner, Irene beaming at everyone finally meeting her charming, successful fiancé, most of dinner spent with family members peppering Grant with questions about what it was like to "be on TV" and to "talk to famous people," all of which Grant seemed to eat right up, along with the prime rib and buttered mashed potatoes, getting uproarious laughter when he stood up to go to the bathroom and said, "I'll be right back after this short break."

"Did you guys see the thing I said at the end of last night's broadcast?" Grant said as he led them to the living room, which was small and cozy, with leather chairs, end tables and a coffee table that looked more expensive than anything Andy had ever owned, and a stone fireplace between bookshelves with titles like *A New Earth* and *The Bartender's Bible* and various awards Grant had won over the years. Several family members—Uncle Lyle and Farah, Uncle Bill and his two kids—were sitting, eating food from paper plates and drinking from plastic cups. Grandma Agnes, Andy and Taylor's dad's mom, sat in the chair to the right of the TV, staring into space, a permanent scowl on her face.

There was something that happened to some old people's faces, where they morphed into a constant look of annoyance, as if like other parts of the body the facial muscles just stopped fully functioning, leaving the mouth in a droopy look of scorn.

Grant again fingered the watch on his left hand.

"No. What'd you say?" Taylor said.

"Oh." Grant seemed surprised. He consulted the time on his watch. "I just said a quick R.I.P. for your parents. Well, here, I DVR'ed it."

He stepped over to the, at least, seventy-inch TV, which was showing a baseball game, and grabbed the remote and pulled up his queue of recorded programs.

"Hey!" Lyle said from a leather chair in the corner. "We were watching that—"

"Just a minute, Lyle. I want to show them the end of last night's broadcast."

"But—"

"Just be a minute."

"It was a nice thing what Grant did," Farah said, her mouth and fork hovering over a small mound of potato salad on her plate.

"Thank you."

"Okay, okay. Sorry. Excuse me," Lyle said, taking a swig from a beer bottle, before setting it on the arm of the chair.

"Coaster, Lyle," Grant said. He located last night's broadcast in the queue.

"Oop! Right. Sorry."

Lyle leaned toward the end table, took another swig of beer, and then set it down on a stone coaster that said *Michigan*, Grant's alma mater.

Grant fast-forwarded through the broadcast, shots of his and the co-anchor's faces speeding by, along with footage of a siren, a body outline, a bundle of balloons, and crime-scene tape.

"Okay, here it is," Grant said.

"—thanks, Jay. And before we say goodnight," TV Grant said, tilting his head and looking forlorn, "if I could take a moment to honor the memory of my wife's aunt and uncle who passed away earlier this week right here in our very city. They will be truly, *truly* missed." The female co-anchor reached over, placing a comforting hand on his arm. TV Grant curled up his lower lip as if he might cry. "Take care of yourselves, Chicago." And then his face transformed into a friendly grin, his booming voice all of a sudden sounding lighter and with more bounce. "And we'll see you tomorrow, bright and early, with our Saturday Morning Team. Goodnight, everyone." TV Grant smiled, and the shot switched to an aerial view of the city at night, car headlights floating across the screen.

Some sniffling passed through the living room.

"Oh, that was really nice, Grant," Farah said. "Very proud of you."

"Yeah," Uncle Bill said.

"Very sweet."

"Is that woman the one that had the nose job?" one of Andy's cousins said.

"No, that was Cindy Wallace, the black one," the other cousin said.

"*African-American.*"

"They prefer 'black.' "

"Okay, kids," Uncle Bill said, digging his hand in the bowl of pretzels on the coffee table.

"Very sweet," Farah said again.

"Thanks, Grant," Candice said.

"Yeah, thanks," Andy said, though on the inside he was rolling his eyes.

"You're very welcome," Grant said to the room. "I know it's not much, but they don't like too much personal stuff on there, but I'm in good with the producers—I would hope so after winning two local Emmys." He shook his arm out, the gold watch jiggling. He looked at the time. "So I thought I could just slip that in." He mimed what looked like fish swimming upstream. "And I did."

"Very nice," Farah said.

"Hey, it's family, so it's important to me," Grant said, nodding.

Irene peaked into the room, the baby still in her arms. "Hey, the dogs are playing in the mud again."

"Jesus Christ," Grant mumbled. "Okay, I'll clean 'em off." He turned to the room. "I'll be back."

"After this short commercial break," Andy said.

"Huh?" Grant said, before heading for the back door.

With Grant outside, Lyle spoke up, "Okay, can someone flip the game back on?"

"Don't be rude," Farah said.

"What? What?"

Taylor, Candice, and Andy walked into the kitchen, where several deli and fruit trays were on the table, along with a pitcher of lemonade, some two-liters of Diet Coke and Sprite, some family pictures, and a bouquet of flowers. Thankfully the urns were nowhere in sight. Where were they? Whose responsibility were those?

"Oh good, you're all here," Aunt Barbara said from near the kitchen sink, where she was talking to Irene and the baby. She smiled.

Andy grabbed a plate and placed on top of it a turkey sandwich on a pretzel bun, some reduced fat Lay's potato chips, and two pieces of watermelon, the whole thing looking practically healthy compared to anything else he had consumed the last few days, save for the Green Giant.

Grant passed through the kitchen with the dogs, this time on a leash.

"I'll put them in the guest room," Grant said to Irene. "Down! Down!" he yelled as Tropper tried to jump up on the table for food.

"That's a good idea," Irene said, holding a bottle to her son's lips.

"They are full of energy, aren't they?" Aunt Barbara said.

Andy found a place to stand in the living room, while Candice and Taylor stayed back in the kitchen, talking to Barbara and Irene.

The baseball game was back on TV.

"Freakin' Verlander blows us away every time," Lyle said, waving his hand at the TV, while his mouth was full with what appeared to be a turkey sandwich. He caught that Andy was in the room. "Oh sorry, son." He got up. "Here, you can have my seat."

"No, that's okay. Thanks."

Lyle shrugged and then sat down, turning his attention back to the TV. "That was a ball! Ugh, terrible. I knew we'd get dicked over with McMahon umping the game."

"Lyle, watch your mouth," Farah said.

"You're right. Sorry."

Grandma Agnes continued her frozen scowl.

Andy spotted the beer in Lyle's hand. He hadn't noticed any beers in the kitchen. Had Lyle brought his own? Lyle had never *seemed* like an alcoholic, other than the fact a beer seemed to always accompany him. But Andy hadn't heard of any problems happening because of this.

Candice came into the room and over to Andy. "Hey. I meant to tell you . . . it's okay you got nervous up there. A lot of people do. I wish Taylor would just ease up." She chewed on a piece of watermelon. "Are you feeling better?"

Andy realized Candice was the first person to ask how he was feeling since his "speech" at the funeral.

"I am. Thanks."

Candice took a bite of her ham sandwich, eyed it, and then set it back on her paper plate, as if having second thoughts.

"That was a ball!" Lyle yelled again.

"*Shhh!*" Farah said.

"Sorry, sorry."

"Can we go home?" Andy's grandma said from her chair, the first words Andy had heard her say.

"In a little bit, mom. A little bit," Lyle said.

Agnes sank further into her chair, clasping her bony fingers together, resigned.

"Hi, grandma," Andy said, walking over to her.

"Wuh? Who said that?"

"It's me. Andrew. Andrew."

"Oh," she said, her scowl almost changing to a smile.

Andy leaned down to hug her, her frail, bony arms shakily grasping his back.

"Awww. Hey, you two, look over here," Farah said, pulling out her cell phone.

Andy got down on one knee near his grandma's chair.

"Wuh?" his grandma said.

"I'm taking your picture," Farah said.

"Oh okay, dear."

Andy smiled.

Farah snapped the photo.

Andy stood up.

"No, one more," Farah said.

Andy lowered himself again, and Farah took the photo.

Andy rose to his feet.

"You look very beautiful, grandma," he said, speaking loudly.

"Oh, you're too sweet. Your wife is one lucky woman. Is she here?"

"No, that's Taylor that's married."

"Oh. Sorry."

"That's okay."

"Is Taylor here?"

"Yes."

"Good. I always liked him. So smart. Or was that you?"

"I'm not sure, grandma," Andy said.

"Do you have a gal?"

Andy paused. "Not really."

"Oh. You should find one. It would make me proud."

"I'd like to do that."

"Good. Thank you, dear." She took a deep breath, her whole body rattling.

Andy looked down at her, lost on what to say next.

"Well, it's good to see you," he finally said.

"You too, dear." She looked into the distance, her face returning to its scowl.

Andy returned to the kitchen.

"Oh good!" Aunt Barbara said, intercepting him before he could take a second trip through the food line (maybe it was better if he didn't get more food, actually). She separated from Irene. "I've been wanting to speak to this stranger." She playfully squeezed Andy's arm.

"Hi, Aunt Barb."

"How are you doing, Andrew? Really."

Andy sighed. "I'm doing . . . okay. I don't think it's hit me yet exactly."

"Oh. All it's done is hit me. Over and over again. My sister. Gone." She pulled her hand to her chest.

"Yeah, it's tough."

"Well," Aunt Barbara said, wiping her eyes. "It was nice to see so many people came. That's not always the case—oh dear, I remember Bill's mother's funeral; it was certainly not the case there. Your parents were loved people. I hope we can all be so lucky."

"Yeah." And then an idea entered Andy's mind. "Do you know Skip Potter?"

Aunt Barbara seemed to stiffen.

". . . Yes, I do—or *did*."

"Did you see him? At the funeral?"

"Um . . . yes. Yes, I did."

"Okay."

"Why?"

Andy shrugged. "Just curious. I know he was an old family friend that I hadn't seen in a while."

"Never thought I'd see him again, but—I mean, it was a surprise is all."

"Why? Did something happen between him and my parents?"

She shook her head quickly. "Nothing, dear. Nothing. Just . . . adult stuff." She waved her hand, as if shooing the whole thing away.

Andy was aware that even though he too was an adult, "adult stuff" somehow still excluded him.

He was about to ask a follow-up question when she said, "Will you excuse me? I told Bill I'd be gone for just a moment."

She brushed past Andy and walked out of the kitchen, where Andy soon realized he was now alone. He leaned against the kitchen counter, the sounds of the baseball game and Lyle's belligerent comments coming from the living room.

Suddenly it seemed clear.

He walked into the living room, where Aunt Barbara was nowhere in sight, and stepped over to Taylor.

"Hey, I realized I left something in your car," Andy said. "Can I get your keys?"

"What'd you forget?"

"Just something. I'll be back."

Taylor eyed him but dug into his pocket and pulled out his keys, handing them to Andy.

Outside, Andy hurried down the street, peeking over his shoulder, worried someone might be watching him. When he made it to Taylor's car, he opened the driver-side door and got inside. Once the key was in the ignition, he looked around the area once more and then turned the key, firing up the car, and drove off.

13

Andy let himself in Taylor and Candice's apartment, using Taylor's key. The apartment was dark and quiet, the shades down. It almost felt like he was trespassing. In a way, he was.

He walked over to the boxes from his parents' house and began looking through them, marveling at some of the things Taylor had kept . . . a macramé lamp shade . . . a garden trowel . . . a coffee mug full of pens, the mug with the word "Yosemite" on the side in an orange and brown font. . . . He made it through the first two boxes in a few minutes. Next was the box with "Andy" written on the side, which he quickly set aside, because the thing he was looking for wasn't in there. Finally, in the bottom box, there it was sitting under a portrait of Andy's parents from the seventies: his parents' address book, the book Taylor had so inexplicably taken.

He stacked all the boxes on top of each other, doing his best to make it look like they hadn't been disturbed. Then, on the floor, he flipped through the address book until he made it to the Ps, where he saw an entry for Skip & Evelyn Potter written in cursive, his mom's handwriting. It must've been written decades ago, his mom buoyantly gripping the black pen as she entered the address of their new, soon to be close, friends.

Andy drove to the house several miles away, coasting down the street with his eyes out the passenger window, like a burglar looking for his next target.

When he saw the number that matched the address in the book, he pulled up to the curb. He looked out the window another time, double-checking, triple-checking the number near the front door. This was the one. Whether they still lived there or not.

His heart was racing as he closed the driver-side door. He didn't have much of a plan, but thinking about it too much would've only weakened his resolve or perhaps made him talk himself out of it.

He walked up the short sidewalk to the large brick house. The house looked almost familiar. Was it? He had probably been here as a kid for a barbecue or Fourth of July party or something, the kids chasing each other with squirt guns, entertaining themselves for hours with these seemingly life-or-death games of chase and war, while the parents clutched Budweisers and talked about work, occasionally yelling at the kids to behave or share.

On the brick front porch, Andy rang the doorbell, which chimed three times.

Ding-dong-DINGGGG

The mailbox was red and said 107.

I LOOK LIKE YOU

There was a speck of mud on the corner of the front porch.

The door opened, and it was Skip. His eyebrows jumped, and he took a step back before grabbing onto the door, holding it half-open.

"*Andrew*. Hi."

"Hi," Andy squeaked out. The sick feeling from the funeral crept up his throat. He rocked slightly forward before regaining his footing. Why did his body have to be so dramatic? He swallowed, though nothing had resurfaced in his mouth.

"Are you feeling all right?" Skip said.

"I saw you at the funeral."

"Oh." Skip looked down for a moment, still gripping the door. "I am terribly, terribly sorry for what happened to your parents. I've been sick about it since I heard. They were very special to me. Practically a second family."

Andy rocked a little forward.

Skip's brow furrowed. "Do you want to come in? Let me get you a glass of water or—"

"No, that's okay."

". . . Okay then."

"Mr. Potter. . . ."

"Yes? And please, you can call me Skip now. You're an adult. Crazy. I remember when you were born." He scratched at his thinning white hair. "I remember—"

"Are you my dad?" Andy clenched and unclenched his hands. His heart pounded.

He saw the piece of mud on the corner of the front porch. It was more than a speck.

Skip's eyes grew wide. "What? What? What could you possibly be talking about? Let me get you some water. You appear sick—"

"I found the note."

"What note? Andrew, are you . . . okay? I know you must be—"

"There was a note in my mom's piggy bank from a Skip. The message and date implied . . . well . . . that this Skip person is my father."

Skip slowly ran his tongue over his teeth, as if computing this, and then glanced over his shoulder, before stepping outside, shutting the door behind him.

He bunched up his shoulders as the cool breeze whipped through his thin white hair.

"Andrew, I don't know what you think—you're under a lot of stress and grief and—"

"Are you my father?" Andy's voice cracked. He cleared his throat. He scratched at his cheek.

The mud on the front porch looked fresh.

Skip again glanced around, as if afraid the neighbors could hear. He wiped at his nose.

Andy continued, "I'm not asking for money, I'm not asking for anything. I just need to know."

Skip winced and then squinted at Andy.

"No, I'm not. I am not your father."

"You're lying. You are lying. I even look like you."

Some day Andy would look just like this man before him, thin white hair being pushed around like leaves of a tree during a cool wind, small hands with gray hairs on the fingers, a weak chin, a slight slouch in his posture.

"Andrew, I think it's best you leave. I'm terribly sorry for what happened. It'll take some time. Just give it time."

Skip turned and reached for the doorknob, opening the door.

"Why did my parents stop talking to you fifteen years ago? What happened?"

Now standing inside the house, with his hand still on the outer doorknob, as if it were holding him up, Skip said, "That's none of your business," and then shut the door.

The deadbolt clicked.

Andy stood there another moment, waiting, waiting, as if expecting Skip might return, and between clenched eyes, admit the truth, but there was nothing. Finally, Andy reached down, and like a child finger-painting, grabbed the hunk of mud—why he had become so obsessed with it, he didn't know—and smeared it over Skip's red wooden door, just a simple slash, a diagonal line, a childish temper tantrum really, but something that just felt right.

And then he heard grass rustling on the side of the house, and a woman emerged from around the corner, wearing gardening gloves and a visor. She saw Andy and gasped, her eyes growing wide. She stopped in place.

Evelyn Potter.

"Excuse me? Can I help you?" She retreated a step. Like Skip, Andy hadn't seen her in probably fifteen years. "Who, who are you?"

"I . . . I. . . ."

She saw the slash of mud on the front door. Her eyes grew wider.

"Skip! Skip!" she called out. She stepped back farther. "Skip! *Skip!*"

Andy started backtracking before speeding up into a hurried walk, Evelyn Potter still shrieking, gesticulating wildly. Over his shoulder, he heard the front door open and Skip come out.

"*What is it? What?*" Skip yelled.

Andy reached the car, fumbling with Taylor's keys.

"Oh, that's just . . . someone probably selling something. Shhh. Shhhhh," Andy heard Skip say before Andy got inside the car, closed the door, and sped off, looking in the rearview mirror and seeing Skip embracing his wife, a look of fear still on her face, while a look of scorn was on Skip's as he watched the car zoom down the street.

14

Andy realized he was still speeding long out of sight of Skip and Evelyn Potter. It was only when he, out loud, said, "Slow down" that he did so, his body still shaking as he gripped the steering wheel with both hands.

He looked down at the gas gauge, seeing there was three-fourths of a tank left. What if he just kept driving? Just found the nearest highway and went with it? There were multiple cities within a few hours. Milwaukee, Iowa City, Madison. He could even go the eight hours back to Kansas City.

And he began to do so, pulling onto the highway and driving a mile or two, still unsure his destination, before he realized how melodramatic he was being, how immature, so he took the next exit and pointed the car toward Irene's house, driving a little more tentatively this time.

When he pulled into a spot in front of Irene's, many of the other cars having left, he saw Taylor and Candice sitting on the front step, both looking dour with their long faces and black dress clothes, their slack postures implying they had probably been sitting there in annoyed silence for a while. Andy's phone had buzzed numerous times in the last hour—probably Taylor—but he had ignored each buzz in his right hip pocket.

Andy turned off the car and got out, just as Taylor rose to his feet, suddenly energized, and charged down the lawn, his right index finger jutting in the air, like an emphatic conductor trying to stir his orchestra into a loud, aggressive volume.

"You fucking stole our car! Where did you go? That's fucking theft! You are a *thief!*"

"Oh shut up," Andy said, heading straight toward his brother, whom he pushed with such force Taylor stumbled backward, his arms swinging and flailing, before he fell onto a patch of muddy grass, his body hitting the earth with a solid *thud*, grass and mud kicking up.

"Stop!" Candice said. "Stop!"

"Oh, butt out of it," Andy said.

Candice's jaw lowered.

Andy took a step back, wincing.

Taylor rose to his feet. "You are insane. You are insane." He brushed himself off, but some mud remained on his pants and jacket.

"Skip Potter is our dad," Andy said, "I just talked to him."

"What? Seriously, just quit it!" Taylor shouted.

"I mean, he denied it," Andy said, momentarily losing his resolve, "but I know it. He's our father. And you denying it, ha, you're just like him. Just like *Dad*."

"Stop with your little theories. You always thought you were better than us, and you're using this weekend to tear down what's left of our family."

Andy, still breathing heavily, stared at his brother.

"Whatever, man," he said. "If you can't accept the truth, you can't accept it. I guess there's no changing you." Calmed down a bit, he turned to Candice. "Candice, look. Sorry I just—"

Taylor sprinted toward him, pushing Andy to the ground, the two brothers grappling, their arms flying, legs kicking.

"Stop! Stop!" Candice continued shouting.

They rolled around on the muddy grass—when had it rained?—the heel of Taylor's palm shoving into Andy's chin, pushing his head back, Andy's knee digging into Taylor's stomach. It was the most physical contact they had had in years.

And then Andy felt his body get lifted up, and Taylor's rose too, as if they were marionettes brought to life, and Andy realized it was the bear grip of Uncle Lyle pulling him up, while Grant had hoisted Taylor to his feet, the two of them holding the Canton twins apart.

When had they come outside?

Candice just looked on, shocked.

"What in the hell are you guys doing?" Lyle said, breathing noisily, his massive arms around Andy's chest, Andy also panting heavily.

Farah was standing on the nearby front step, looking equally stunned. She was holding onto Grandma Agnes who stared into space, the scowl still on her face, probably not computing what was going on, but it was enough to make Andy flinch again, feeling extra exposed, extra embarrassed.

"I . . . We. . . ." Andy said, before his voice faded out.

At Taylor and Candice's apartment, the three of them again fell into separate silences, Taylor retreating to his laptop at the kitchen table, while Candice hurried to the bedroom, closing the door behind her, claiming she needed to "lie down." Andy found refuge in the bathroom. After a shower he tended to his suit, scrubbing out the mud and dirt stains. Luckily he could still wear it to the wedding. The wedding tonight—at least he had that.

He emerged from the bathroom at 5:00, having been in there over an hour.

Taylor looked up from his seat at the kitchen table, annoyed. He wasn't wearing his glasses.

"Where are you going?" he said.

"A wedding."

Taylor let out a single chuckle, baffled. "You have got to be kidding me."

"I met a girl a couple nights ago, and now I'm going to a wedding with her."

Taylor threw up his hands and shook his head. "You are fucking ridiculous. We have other family stuff to deal with. Several decisions we have to make about mom and dad's estate. You're lucky I'm even letting you be a part of it after—"

"You know what: *you* handle it. You can make the decisions. I don't care anymore."

"Yeah, you never did. Jesus."

"Well, maybe you should show a little more care for your own wife."

"What are you talking about?"

"I'm just saying, man . . . if I had a wife, I'd give her a little more attention and care."

Taylor scoffed. "As if you know anything about marriage, let alone a long-term adult relationship."

"You're right, I don't. But being married doesn't all of a sudden make you an expert on love either."

Taylor shook. "Just get the fuck out of here and go to your stupid wedding."

"Gladly."

"I think you and I are done."

"I couldn't agree more."

Andy grabbed his wallet from the table and headed out the door, pulling it tight behind him, it smacking hard against the frame.

15

A ndy climbed the stairs, along with the other wedding guests, to the second floor of the Glenn Event Space. Once through the doorway, things opened into a large space, with wood floors and brick walls—it looked like a downtown loft, really, one of those industrial buildings that had been refurbished and turned into office and event space. The floor creaked with age. There were exposed pipes and ducts. It smelled like wood and steel. And on the far end of the room was a picture window overlooking the busy Chicago streets below.

Andy surveyed the decorations specific to the wedding: red and white flower petals on the floor, as if a flower girl had already sprinkled some around; pictures of the couple, her engagement ring prominently displayed in several of the photos, the girl with long blonde hair with brown tips, while the guy's hair was already receding; large lights hanging from the ceiling, dimmed to give an intimate, cozy feel—all making Andy think the Stoddard could stand to catch up, as their lighting and decorations were good but hardly to this level. He made a mental note to bring it up at next week's managerial meeting.

Maybe he wasn't a "big deal" at the Stoddard, but maybe he could change that.

The Stoddard hosted several weddings a year. Weddings were a mixed bag there, as they must be at any hotel. On the one hand, it meant a lot of money, not to mention publicity for the wedding guests seeing the Stoddard for the first time. Plus, many wedding guests stayed the night in the hotel, splurging on expensive rooms, room service, and other things—but therein lay the problem, the guests exiting the banquet hall after the wedding, stumbling around the halls like drunk zombies from *Night of the Living Dead*—they didn't have to drive home, so they could get as drunk as they wanted—tripping drunkenly on the stairs and then trying to blame the hotel for "negligence," riding the elevators up and down for hours like children, loudly singing Jay Z lyrics outside their rooms at 2:00 a.m., causing other hotel guests to call the front desk to complain, Andy having to launch into full-on appeasement mode. On multiple occasions, he had had to call security on a guest peeing in a potted plant.

Andy turned his attention to his own appearance. He touched the knot of his tie, making sure it had just the right looseness. If he were at work, he would've buttoned the top button, pulling the tie snug—the Stoddard could be rather conservative when it came to dress—but he wasn't at work, so he left the top button undone. He checked that his silver tie clip was straight. He checked his belt. Some dust or dirt had gotten on his left shoe, probably while he was on the L train here, the other passengers tracking in something from outside, so he bent over, brushing it off.

He peered around the room again, hoping to see Shannon, but she was probably off with the bridesmaids somewhere getting ready. So much went into bridesmaids getting ready, while groomsmen getting ready mostly meant popping the top off beers and frantically putting on your suit five minutes before walking down the aisle.

Andy stepped over to the makeshift chapel near the picture window, an altar at the front with a microphone on a microphone stand, and rows of white chairs split down the center like a sanctuary. A few dozen people were here already, some sitting in the chairs or standing in groups, some talking, some just looking at cell phones. Andy checked his watch—the ceremony started in fifteen minutes.

An usher walked up to him. He appeared a few years younger, with a beard that looked like it took time and careful grooming. His hair was slicked back, tall on top and short on the sides. The guy looked sharp, Andy thought, almost like an affront on his own appearance, like in addition to the Stoddard's banquet hall lighting and decoration needs, Andy too needed to step it up. Maybe he could squeeze in some shopping before leaving tomorrow.

"Are you with the bride's side or the groom's?" the usher said.

Andy blanked. He wasn't with any of them. In a way, he felt like he was crashing the wedding.

Shannon and he hadn't even talked today, Shannon texting him all the details last night. Hopefully she hadn't had second thoughts about his coming. Should he have texted for confirmation today?

"Bride's," Andy finally said.

The usher handed him a program and pointed to the left rows of seats. Andy began walking, assuming he'd be taking it from here, but the usher walked with him. Why able-bodied people needed help getting to their seats, Andy had no idea.

"So how do you know Rebecca?" the usher asked.

"Oh, I'm one of the bridesmaids' dates, actually. Yeah, I've never even met her—Rebecca."

"Right on. I barely know her either, but I'm one of Sean's friends from DePaul."

"Oh wow, I went there too. Graduated in '06."

"No shit? '09 for me."

"Nice. Go Blue Demons."

"Ha. Yeah."

Andy stopped at a row around the middle of the makeshift chapel. Not too close, not too far back.

"Is here okay?" Andy said, pointing to the aisle seat.

"Absolutely. Oh man, awesome shoes by the way." He pointed down.

"Oh yeah? Thanks, man. I was gonna say the same thing about your suit. Where'd you get that? Sorry, I'm kind of clothes-obsessed."

The guy laughed, stroking his beard. "No problem. Me too."

Andy smiled. This room of strangers was already more enjoyable than all the family time he had had this weekend.

The usher continued, "Banana Republic actually. Yeah, I know, what a sell-out."

"That's expensive stuff."

"I know, I know. Fuck. I'm not rich, I swear."

"It looks good. I've been wanting to try a checkered gray like that." Andy suddenly felt boring for wearing a predictable black suit to the wedding— well, he hadn't known when he packed that he'd have a wedding to go to.

"Thanks. Yeah, I like it a lot. Thanks. Well . . . right on. Well, I'm Derek."

"Andy."

They shook hands.

"We'll talk more later," Derek said, patting Andy on the shoulder and returning to the back of the chapel to usher more people to their seats.

Andy took a seat, feeling lighter. Though he lived a so-called liberal life in regard to his views and his friends, having a conversation about style and fashion with other men had always seemed to make most guys (him too) a little nervous, that no matter how non-homophobic or progressive you were, the fact you gave a shit about your looks and what you wore could give off a "weak" vibe, could make you seem less of a quote-unquote *man*. Whatever.

He looked at the program Derek had handed him. On the front was flowy, over-the-top cursive that said, once Andy had stared at it long enough and could finally make it out: *Mr. and Mrs. Sean and Rebecca Harkins*, with two doves holding up their names. The inside used a more legible font, listing the order of the ceremony and the names of the attendants, including Shannon Petrovski. "Petrovski" was her last name? What was that? Russian? Czech? Polish?

Having thoroughly read through the program, Andy turned his attention to the front corner, where a guy in black pants and a white shirt with blue stripes was looking at a Macbook connected to large speakers. He was playing some background music, Explosions in the Sky type stuff, ambient and quiet. DJs played music at ceremonies? Taylor and Candice's had been more traditional, a piano player and organist playing the standard wedding pieces, a live band at the reception playing Earth, Wind & Fire, Michael Jackson, etc.

Would Taylor ever get married again?

Would Andy ever get married at all?

And what about his relationship with Taylor? Really, he didn't feel like ever talking to him again— what good could come of that?—but maybe completely cutting off things with your twin was like cutting off a body part—there'd always be a phantom limb there, an absence that would pester you your whole life. It was a begrudging realization that he needed to patch things up with Taylor, that frustrating moment when what you *need* to do doesn't match with what you'd *prefer* to do. He'd prefer to do jack shit. Let Taylor piss and whine. But they needed to work out some sort of compromise. They needed to have a good relationship.

But how?

At a few minutes after 6:00, members of the wedding party started walking down the aisle. A few people back was Shannon in a light purple dress, her hand on the arm of a groomsman with a large goatee. She spotted Andy and smiled, giving his shoulder a quick squeeze as she passed by.

Andy zoned out during the ceremony, mostly just staring at Shannon—she looked really pretty, her hair done up in a bun, her thin fingers holding a bouquet near her waist, her makeup applied at, what seemed like, the right level, while some of the other bridesmaids looked clownish with their pink cheeks and heavily-colored eyelids. When the . . . pastor? minister? officiant? said, "You may now kiss the bride," and the guests began clapping, Andy snapped out of his daze, joining them in their raucous applause at two people kissing in front of them.

The newly-minted Harkins walked up the aisle, Rebecca raising her hand holding the bouquet, while Sean high-fived some people on the aisle seats, the bridal party exiting after them, and Andy this time nudged Shannon with a playful fist to her exposed shoulder, Shannon responding with a flirty look over her shoulder, before she continued walking up the aisle.

Tonight. . . .

An excitement stirred up inside him, like a slow shock of electricity passing through his body. It felt more than the pleasant buzz of "I might get laid tonight," but that for one night he might not obsess over his diet, his clothes, his body, the smudges on hotel front doors, but only having a good time and making sure someone else did too.

Andy walked up to Shannon near the back of the room, where the other guests were milling around after the ceremony, while the makeshift chapel was being flipped into a spot for the reception, tables set up and tablecloths draped over them like bed sheets, the whole thing carried out like a quick military display.

She greeted him with a hug. Her perfume was strong but nice.

"You smell good," he said.

"Thanks."

He was looking forward to getting in the, now, long line for drinks at the bar near the middle of the room, getting her whatever she felt like, while he got a whiskey and soda for himself, and then perhaps suggesting they stand over by the large picture window and look over the busy streets below. It was getting dark outside, and the downtown lights were coming on. That, mixed with the car headlights slowly moving, gave the streets a glow. But then one of the bridesmaids came over. It took Andy a second to remember her name . . . Keely.

"Hey, Shan, we got to take pictures."

"Oh, right," Shannon said, frowning, before turning to Andy. "We'll be back in, like, an hour, I think." She pinched his hip before walking away.

"Oh . . . okay," Andy said, but she was already out of earshot.

Andy peered down at his shoes for a second and then got in the long line for drinks, everyone having seemingly raced to the bar once the ceremony ended. He glanced at his watch, even though what time it was meant little. He'd be in this line for a while.

"Oh hey man," Andy heard over his shoulder.

He turned around, seeing Derek behind him.

"Mind if I join you in line?" Derek said.

"No, not at all."

"My girlfriend's over in the corner taking selfies with her friends, so that'll be probably half an hour before they're done or whatever."

"Ha. True. Which one's your girlfriend?"

"She's the one . . . you see the one in the black dress with the . . . spaghetti straps or linguini straps or whatever they're called . . . kind of leaning down a bit?"

"Yeah. Cool. Nice."

"Yeah, she's pretty great," Derek said. "I mean, I don't know." He chuckled. "It's tough, y'know?"

"Oh yeah."

"So what about you and . . . sorry, what's her name?"

"Shannon? Honestly I've known her two days."

Derek's eyebrows jumped..

"We're both from out of town," Andy continued. "Just having a little fun, I guess. I don't mean that in a perverted way. But she seems pretty cool. I know this is a weird thing to say, but people love it when they have the same likes as someone else.

Well, Shannon and I seem to have that, but we also seem to have the same hates too, which is kind of fun."

Derek laughed.

"I don't know," Andy said, shaking his head. "I probably shouldn't say much more. I don't want to jinx it."

"Understandable, man. Let's get a drink."

After they got their drinks, they walked away from the bar.

"Hey, you don't mind if I join you for a bit?" Andy said. "I don't mean to keep bugging you, but Shannon's off taking photos with the wedding party."

"Not at all. Definitely join us. You're not bugging me. Here, I'll introduce you to everyone."

Derek led him to a group of similarly well-dressed people, clutching drinks, both girls holding handbags, one of the guys with tall black hair, wearing an awesome-looking watch on his right wrist. Their names came at Andy quickly: Chelsey and her boyfriend Tom. Derek's girlfriend Layla. Seong, the guy with the watch.

Andy shook their hands, them smiling back at him, not appearing annoyed to have this stranger joining their group.

After introductions, someone asked Andy what he did.

"I'm a manager at a hotel." He left the "night" part off. It sounded better without it.

"No shit? I bet you have some good stories," Derek said.

"Yeah, I got a few," Andy said, laughing, and then took a sip of his drink.

"Well?" Seong said.

"Well. . . ." Andy rocked back on his heels. "I guess it depends what you want: drugs, sex, or violence?"

"Drugs," Layla said, giggling over her vodka cranberry.

"Okay, okay. Let's see . . . okay." Andy took another sip of his drink and looked up, all their attention on him. "There was this guy who would check in under a false name, like Robert something. We never knew, because that was the name on his credit card too, but apparently it was some sketchy account or whatever. Anyway, he'd come in for just a night, like every couple weeks or so. I figured he was just another guy meeting a hooker or a mistress or whoever at the hotel. And there'd always be a package waiting for him that had come to the hotel a day or two before. It was always kind of weird, like, why is he getting mail at the hotel for these very short stays, but it's none of our business, I guess. And he always paid on time and was super nice and all those things, so I kind of thought, whatever, it's no big deal."

Andy looked around the group, noticing everyone was still staring at him with apparent full attention. It was almost unheard of these days to stand in a group of people and not see at least one person resorting to their cell phone for entertainment, the nervous twitch of his generation. But maybe these people standing before him were different. Cool.

"So," he continued, "one day, one of the maids went to clean his room. There was no 'Do Not Disturb' sign on his door, and when she knocked no one answered, so she went right in, and there was the guy hunched over a mirror on the bed, several lines of coke laid out, a rolled twenty-dollar bill up his nose. Apparently he flipped out but just tried to stand in front of the coke. Anyway, long story short, we called the cops, drug-sniffing dogs came in, etc. It was pretty entertaining, though one of the dogs took a shit in the hallway."

The group laughed.

"That's awesome."

"*So* funny."

"Ha. Nice."

"What a bozo."

"I know," Andy said, smiling.

"So, come on," Seong said, "what else? What other stories?"

"Oh," Andy said. "Well—I mean, I don't mean to hog the conversation. So what do you all—"

"No, please," Derek said.

"It's either you or Tom talking about his Instagram," Layla said.

"What," Tom laughed, "I take cool photos!"

The whole group laughed.

"So okay," Chelsey said, "sex this time."

"Okay, sure," Andy said, before he launched into another story from the hotel, the whiskey settling in nicely, his whole body and mind just feeling good, surrounded by these people who seemed genuinely interested in him, and Shannon back from photos in half an hour, that playful hip pinch still replaying in his mind—this last night in Chicago perhaps being something, something really good.

Please.

When Shannon returned, a water in her hand, Andy introduced her to the group, them welcoming her like they had him.

"These people are awesome," Andy said, sounding almost drunk even though he didn't think he was.

"And this guy's awesome," Tom said, pointing at Andy.

"He is," Shannon said.

Andy smiled.

"All right," the DJ said in a low voice on the microphone. "If we could have everyone find their seats, our father of the bride is going to lead us in a grace before we begin dinner. Thanks!"

"Oh god," Layla said.

"Literally," Chelsey said.

"Unfortunately, I think we're seated at another table," Shannon said to Andy and the group.

"Really?" Andy said, his smile fading.

"Well, hey, let's exchange numbers," Derek said.

"Okay. Yeah!" Andy said, perhaps a little too loudly.

Andy passed his phone around, each of them entering their name and number. In reality he didn't know when he'd use the numbers—they all lived in

Chicago; he didn't. But it was still nice to think he could.

During dinner, Andy sat at a table with Shannon and a few other members of the wedding party, while the bride and groom sat at their own table in the center of the dance floor, as if an attraction at a zoo, a tiny table where they both looked nervous and awkward, gaping out at everyone, as they forked food into their mouths.

Shannon and Andy's table was covered in water, champagne, and alcohol glasses, beer bottles, bread plates, dinner plates, and a round centerpiece of fake flowers and twigs, with a picture in the middle of Rebecca and Sean holding hands on a beach somewhere, the photo pointing right at Andy, their smiling faces watching him eat.

It didn't take long to realize Andy and Shannon were the odd ones out, everyone else at the table seeming to have become friends long before this weekend, and to have a rapport about the University of Illinois, reality TV, and the pros and cons of vacationing in Mexico, all things Andy knew little about, and he doubted Shannon did either.

When one of them asked how Andy and Shannon knew each other, Keely piped in before either could respond.

"Oh, I know the answer. He met her at this bar we were at a couple days ago. Shannon was sick, sitting by herself, and Andy swooped right in, the creeper."

Andy didn't know whether to laugh or be insulted—her face didn't give any clues—so he laughed along with everyone else, faking it.

The guy sitting to his left—Barry? Brent? Brad?—playfully punched Andy in the arm, it actually stinging a bit. "That's how we do it, man," the guy said with a mouthful of chicken.

"Ha. Yeah."

"So what made you approach her?" one of the bridesmaids asked.

"The guy's got a penis, doesn't he?" her boyfriend said. He took in her look. "What? What? Am I wrong?"

"Last time I checked I had one," Andy said.

The table laughed, Andy wanting to shrink away and take Shannon with him.

"So ignoring my dumbass boyfriend, what made you approach her? I'm just curious how men's minds work."

They don't, Andy wanted to say, *just look at your boyfriend for proof.*

"She had that 'I'm about to throw up' look that I find irresistible," Andy finally said, running his hand over her back.

Shannon mimed throwing up onto her plate.

Andy placed his hand on her bun of hair.

"Got your hair, babe."

Andy and Shannon laughed but heard mostly scattered, fading laughter in return.

One of the guys said, "So wait—"

"Ohhh, you're joking," one of the bridesmaids said.

Her boyfriend rolled his eyes.

And then everyone fell into their own conversations again.

Andy pulled out his phone and typed a text to Shannon: *You're awesome. These people are...*

He handed his phone to her. She read what he had written and smiled, and then typed a few letters before returning the phone to him.

...the worst!

They laughed. She placed her hand on his leg, rubbing it gently. He placed his hand on her back. Whatever skittishness or hesitance she had been feeling last night—the shying away after the short kiss, the reluctance to invite him up—she seemed more than pleased to be in his company tonight, it all just making Andy really, really happy.

After Rebecca and Sean cut the cake, and the caterers quickly sliced up pieces, dishing them out onto small plates, the DJ announced that guests could help themselves to a slice. Several people immediately darted over, a similar urgency to when the bar had opened after the ceremony. Cake: loaded to the brim with sugar and chemicals with numbers in their names, but Andy felt like, *why the hell not*, so he stood up.

"You want a piece?" he said to Shannon.

"Yeah. That'd be nice. Thank you."

"What a charmer," said one of the guys at their table.

In line behind the more eager guests, Andy was joined by Keely.

"Hey, take good care of her," she said. She looked over her shoulder at Shannon sitting thirty feet away at their table.

"I will. I mean, we're just"—Andy shrugged—"y'know, hanging out for the weekend." Whether that was entirely true or not, he still didn't know. Really, he was just sick of everyone at their table inquiring about his relationship with Shannon. It made him feel like he was on trial. Why were they all so curious?

"She just seems a little . . . how do I say this . . . delicate."

"How so?" Andy said.

"Well, I've only known her a few days, but she's always, like, crying and running off. She looked terrible when I first saw her today."

"Really?"

"I'm just saying, if you're just using her for sex, just don't. Just . . . Shannon seems fragile."

"No, I mean—we haven't had . . . sex. We've just, y'know, kissed, like, once. Really, it'll be okay."

". . . Okay then," Keely said, still appearing skeptical. She walked away, leaving the line, before glancing over her shoulder one more time at Andy, her expression serious and unrelenting.

Later, Shannon and Andy were standing and talking, both happy to be away from their dinner companions, Andy holding a beer—his third, no *fourth*, of the night—while Shannon nursed a Sprite, when the DJ started playing Boyz II Men's "I'll Make Love To You." Andy looked at the DJ who was standing and grooving, rocking side to side like he was slow dancing with himself.

"This reminds me of sixth grade," Andy said.

"A song about fucking?"

"You wanna dance?" Andy cracked his voice on purpose, sounding like a pubescent boy.

"Just as long as you never do that voice again."

"Deal."

They finished their drinks and headed to the floor, Andy putting his arms around Shannon's waist and Shannon placing hers over his shoulders.

"I think this is closer than I ever got to a girl in sixth grade. Or ninth grade, for that matter," he said.

"Occasionally I'll see thirteen-year-olds in public, holding hands, and I just want to yell at them," Shannon said. "Like, 'you're too young!' Even though when I was that age, I wanted to do all those things and feel grown-up and stuff. I was reading *Cosmo* already and wondering what 'trigger spots' meant."

"I know. Ugh. Have we become the lame older people who think kids are hooking up too young?"

"Well, they are."

"Case in point."

Shannon placed her head on his shoulder.

"Why don't you live in San Francisco?" she said into his chest.

"Why don't you live in Kansas City? Ah, San Francisco's better."

She repositioned her hands on his shoulders, pulling him closer.

Andy felt like he could stand like this for hours.

Damn . . . why didn't they live in the same city?

Over Shannon's shoulder, Andy made eye contact with Keely, who stared back at him—why was she being so hyper-protective of Shannon?

"You wanna get out of here?" Andy finally said.

Shannon lifted up her head. "But I think there's still an hour left."

"Maybe we could see a little more of the city before we both leave tomorrow."

She gave him a mischievous smile. "Well . . . okay. Yeah, let's. I hate Boyz II Men anyway."

Andy grabbed Shannon by the hand, and they hurried to their table to grab their things, and then they said goodbye to the other members of the wedding party, Rebecca and Sean, and Derek and his group of friends, them all making promises to keep in touch, whether it actually happened or not, the whole series of goodbyes occurring in what felt like thirty seconds, before they got outside to the chilly Chicago Spring night, Andy feeling so fucking alive, so *present*, that all the shit before now seemed like truly the past, truly *done*, and anything that might happen the rest of tonight might just be amazing.

16

Shannon and Andy walked a few blocks, holding hands, laughing. She kept herself close to him.

"Did you see the way that DJ was dancing?"

"God, it felt so good to get out of there."

"Rebecca seems cool and all, but—"

"Oh yeah, but it's weddings that can be intolerable."

"Ugh, we're so negative."

"I know! Ah. I'm just thankful at least you were there."

"And that lone table in the middle of the dance floor where Rebecca and Sean sat?"

"They looked so uncomfortable."

"I know!"

"But maybe that still would've been less awkward than our table."

"True."

"I must've had like four Sprites tonight."

"Sugar, sugar, sugar."

"Yum."

"I know."

On the corner of Remington and Dodge, Andy saw a stocked bike rack for PedalPass, the red and white rental bikes he had seen all over the city the last couple days. Kansas City had them too—for seven dollars you could rent a bike for an hour, before returning it at one of the PedalPass bike racks in the city. There were dozens of them.

"Come on," Andy said, pulling Shannon across the street, the two of them dodging a car that honked at them.

"Whoa!"

"Haha."

"You wanna ride bikes?" Shannon said, as Andy hurriedly pulled out his credit card, reading over the instructions on the kiosk.

"Yeah. Why not?"

"I'm in a dress."

Andy looked her over. A tight dress would've made riding a bike almost impossible, but hers was loose and flowy.

"You'll be fine. Come on. I haven't ridden a bike in like fifteen years."

"Neither have I."

"So see, it's perfect. We'll both do something on this trip that we haven't done in a long, long time."

"Hmm. Well okay, I hope you're right."

Andy smiled, and once they grabbed their bikes, unhooking them from the bike racks, fourteen dollars soon to be added to his credit-card statement, they began pedaling—or at least attempting to pedal, the two of them wobbling the handlebars back and forth while they tried to get their bikes going.

"Ha. This is harder than I remember it," Andy said, the bike further proving he was a little drunk, his motor skills not at their peak ability.

"Yikes. Yeah."

But eventually they got up to speed, their handlebars straightening out, their grips becoming less tense, their bikes cruising down the sidewalk and then into the street, which luckily wasn't too busy with cars, their bike wheels spinning fluidly, pushing them forward. Other cyclists passed them, nodding, carrying messenger bags, boxy headphones, and helmets—all of them wearing, what looked to be, more comfortable, bike-appropriate clothes than Shannon's flowy dress and Andy's black suit.

After about ten minutes, as they coasted down Templeton, a residential street with no traffic, the two of them with no real destination in mind, Shannon pulled up beside Andy, giving him a competitive look.

"Oh, you're on," Andy said. He sped up, pumping the pedals harder.

"Ah!" she said, pedaling more aggressively and moving even with him.

"No, no!" he said, swatting at her, causing his bike to wobble and lose even more ground.

She laughed, eluding his attacks.

"Okay, now watch this," she said. She slowed down to become even with him and then let go of the handlebars, holding her arms in the air like a high-wire walker, as she continued pedaling.

"This is amazing," she said.

Andy looked at her and her smile, maybe the biggest he had seen since meeting her two days ago. She didn't look like a girl who had been crying all weekend. She couldn't be. And if she had been crying, she looked like someone over it now. Besides, some girls cried a lot. So what? It could've just been a body thing, a hormonal thing. It wasn't anything to worry about.

And watching her, as she continued pedaling without using her hands, Andy knew they had to see each other again after this weekend.

He'd find a way.

Shannon looked over at Andy, still grinning, and then when she turned back to face the street, she screamed, "Oh shit!" and slammed right into a parked car, her body flying over the top and the hood, landing near the curb.

"Shannon!"

Andy slammed on the brakes, his tires squealing, his bike jerking to a stop, and he rushed over to her, dropping his bike in the street—they should've worn helmets; they shouldn't be riding bikes at midnight; he was making a mess of everything, turning anyone who touched him into death or another form of dying, but all he saw was Shannon lying on the sidewalk, her head in a patch of grass, laughing.

"Oh ow," she said between laughs, rolling from side to side.

Andy dropped to his knees, putting his hands on her shoulders.

"I'm okay," she said. "I think I just skinned my elbow. Ow."

Andy helped her sit up slowly. She shook her head, shaking away the dizziness. She blinked several times. She turned over her right elbow, revealing its scratched exterior, which, though red, didn't appear to be bleeding.

"I got to stop hanging out with you," she said. "We're always crashing—oh, my dress!" Her dress was torn near the bottom, with dirt and grass spots seemingly everywhere. "Whatever, I was never going to wear this again. I hate purple."

She laughed and Andy started laughing too, and they both lay back in the patch of grass, Andy holding Shannon, their bikes still in the middle of the street, road kill if any cars were to come by, but Andy didn't care. He was happy.

17

S hannon lay back on the bed in her hotel room, the comforter thrown off, the sheets in a tangle, the two pillows cradling her head, her face lit only by the subtle glow of the nightstand lamp, as Andy hovered over her.

He smiled and then slid off the straps of her torn and dirty dress.

"Here," he said in a hushed voice. "Roll over."

She smirked and did so, and he grabbed the top of her dress's zipper and slowly pulled it down. When he got to the bottom, she flipped over and said, "Let me help you" and in a quick succession of motions freed herself of the dress, kicking it across the room. "Sorry, you were going too slow."

They both laughed, and she reached up to him, pulling him down, their mouths meeting and fitting together in different combinations like a jigsaw puzzle with a number of connections that, though clumsy, were all right; they all worked.

After a few moments, she pulled her mouth away, and with her hands, grabbed at his shirt buttons. He continued kissing her forehead, their hurried breathing filling the room. Finally she flung his shirt across the room, the two of them giggling like mischievous teenagers up to no good.

He started softly palming her small breasts, still encased in her bra, before he reached around to her back, pawing at the bra hooks, which seemed invented to make it difficult for removal, but he unclasped them in a quick one-two freeing, which every time felt like a victory of man over technology.

Things moved from there, Shannon reaching down, unbuckling Andy's pants and then touching his dick, which grew in hardness, their kissing and breathing increasing in speed and volume.

"I want you inside me. Come on, come on," Shannon said, through clenched eyes. She sounded impatient, ready. But so was Andy.

"Okay, okay," Andy whispered. He grabbed at his pants near the edge of the bed and found his wallet, where one condom resided.

He handed it to her, Shannon quickly tearing off the wrapping like it was a Christmas present, and placed it on Andy's penis, sliding it down.

He laid her back on the bed, resettling her head on the pillows a few inches from the headboard.

Andy got in position in front of her, lifting up her legs, and wedging himself in between, and the trip to Chicago was becoming a success in a way, and the problems with Taylor and his family were just no big deal and would get worked out—of course they'd get worked out. Why stress they wouldn't?—and he was about to enter her, when Shannon placed her hands on his legs, clutching his thighs with urgency, and said, "No, no. Wait."

"Okay, okay." He pulled back.

Shannon, still with her eyes closed, rolled to the side, her legs falling to the bed. She winced. Her shoulder seemed to jerk up, as if a reflex. "I shouldn't do this, I shouldn't—"

"It's okay, it's okay. We don't have to."

"There are things you don't know about me."

"There are things you don't know about me either. It's okay."

Andy reached out to rub her shoulder.

"I haven't told you the whole story," Shannon said, still keeping her eyes closed, Andy's hand going up and down her side. "I'm . . . two-months pregnant."

His hand stopped. He removed it from her side.

Shannon opened her eyes, peering back at Andy, Shannon looking frightened, while Andy's look of empathy and concern descended into shock.

The blood rushed to his head, and he swayed a bit before letting himself fall onto his back next to her. In between his legs, his erection retreated.

"Really," he finally said, flatly.

"It was an accident. My boyfriend and I just got careless one night, and when he found out I'm pregnant—"

"He left you," Andy said, monotone. "And that's why you've been sick this trip. That's why you haven't been drinking."

Shannon nodded, tears forming in her eyes.

"I'm just not available," she said. "I tried to fight it, but I'm not."

And he was just desperate and lonely . . . naked in a bed next to a pregnant woman, feeling robbed by the universe—or by a guy, her ex-boyfriend, whom he didn't know at all.

He was just tired. Tired, tired. Of a lot of things.

The second you care is the second—

"The person I didn't want to see at the barcade," she said, sniffling, ". . . that was the person who told my ex I'm pregnant. Never thought I'd see them in Chicago, hanging out here for some reason. . . . Someone I thought I could trust, but then I learned that wasn't true anymore."

Andy winced. "When were you planning to tell your boyfriend?"

"I don't know. I just needed time. *I* was supposed to be the one to tell him."

Andy stayed silent.

The bed and the room fell still.

He just. . . .

He started sliding off the bed, looking for his clothes.

"I think I better go."

Shannon opened her eyes again. "No, wait, I—"

"Look, I wasn't here just to get laid or anything." He slid on his boxers and pants. "But . . . I gotta go. I'm sorry. I liked you, I really did. Sorry, I'm a little freaked out—"

"No, come on. Can we talk about this? Please?"

He finished buttoning his shirt and peered down at her, her naked body splayed out on the bed, her face looking ashamed and sad in the thin light from the lamp.

"I—yeah, I just better go."

Andy didn't wait to put on his shoes and socks, before he headed toward the door and into the hallway—he could put them on out there—Andy hearing "No, please wait!" coming from the bed as he closed the door, the automatic lock clicking behind him.

There was an impulse to turn around and knock on the door, but no, no.

He walked down the hall, still in his bare feet, carrying his shoes and socks—he just needed to get away; that was the best thing for him now. He'd put them on when he got to the bank of elevators, some seemingly simple task to occupy him as he waited for the *ding* and the elevator doors to open.

A man carrying a Diet Coke walked toward him, going the opposite direction down the hall.

He smirked at Andy. "Ah, looks like you had some fun tonight." He lifted his Diet Coke in a note of *cheers!*, before raising his free hand in a high-five, waiting for Andy's obliging touch. But instead Andy lunged toward him, pushing him against the wall, Andy's shoes and socks dropping from his hands. The Diet Coke fell, crashing to the floor, where it began spilling onto the gray carpet.

"*J*esus!" the guy said, trying to squirm out of Andy's grasp, Andy's left fist grabbing the guy's collar, his right arm pinning the guy against the wall. "What's your problem, man? I was just, *ah*, joking. *J*esus! Let me—go!"

Andy, shaking, let go of the man, surprised at his actions, ready to apologize, to buy the man another Diet Coke, when the guy slapped him hard.

"Ah!" Andy yelled, grasping at his eye as he squatted down, falling to the floor, landing in the puddle of Diet Coke near his shoes and socks.

The guy hurried away. "I ought to call security on your ass! Maniac."

Andy clutched at his face. His eye stung and was tearing up. He could barely open it, his vision now distorted.

A headache pulsed at the back of his head, his shoes and pants now wet with Diet Coke.

Andy put his soaked shoes on, feeling like he didn't give a fuck about the socks, which he stuffed in his pockets as he rose to his feet, stumbling against the wall.

He got in the elevator, thankful no one else was in there, and rode it down to the first floor, where he hobbled toward the front door.

"Good evening, sir," a bellboy said. "Have a nice—whoa, are you okay, dude?"

"I'm fine," Andy said, moving past him.

"Do you need me to call a cab? Let me—"

"No," Andy said, going out the front sliding doors back into the cool Chicago night, realizing he had left his suit coat in Shannon's room.

18

He walked toward his brother's place—annoyed that was his only realistic option for where to sleep tonight—his arms folded, his whole body shivering against the breeze.

His phone buzzed in his pocket, and after a moment of deliberation, he took it out to see a text from Shannon:

We should talk. Please.

He quickly deleted it, jabbing at the screen with urgency. He didn't hate her. But get involved with a pregnant girl? The whole idea was insane.

Andy turned the corner of Baker and Reed, a couple blocks from Taylor's apartment. A few feet away he saw a homeless man sitting on a crate, his back against the side of a Walgreen's, the man bundled up in a dirty blue parka, holding a cardboard sign, even though it was nearly 1:00 a.m. and few people were walking around the street now. Andy glanced over, reading its message: "Homeless and hungry. Please help. I'm not a drug user or a drunk. God bless."

"Mister, any spare change?"

Andy stopped, taking his hands out of his pockets. He turned to the man.

"No, I don't. But how about this . . . why don't you do something with your life, instead of sitting on a milk crate you probably stole from a grocery store—or from Walgreen's right here," Andy said, his heart racing again. "You're clearly capable of writing, you have legible penmanship; how about reading a book or, I don't know, writing on a *job* application for once instead of a piece of cardboard that you similarly probably stole from a dumpster, instead of sitting on your ass doing nothing, begging people who work hard for a living for a piece of their hard-earned money. I know as a democrat, I'm supposed to feel for you, but after a while, it's hard to feel anything but annoyance at yet another person bugging me for a handout."

The man stared back at Andy, his eyes large with fright like the man Andy had shoved against the wall.

Oh god, Andy thought, taking a step back, his breath becoming uneven, his head still aching, his eye squinting and tearing up. He had just said the type of thing his dad would've said—or would've *wanted* to say—Andy's normally nice dad angry at another person wanting a "handout."

. . . But in many ways, this outburst was also pure Andy.

And wait—his "dad" wasn't even his real dad, he remembered. His dad was a flake who was still alive and living a lie some fifteen minutes away.

Andy felt sick.

He pulled out his wallet, fishing out a twenty.

"I'm sorry," Andy said, reaching out, the bill wafting in the breeze.

"No, no. Go. Just go." The homeless man pulled his hands and the sign in between his knees, bracing against the wind or Andy.

"No, I'm sorry. Take it. Please take it."

"No. Please go."

Andy dropped the twenty in front of him, but the man stayed on the crate, shivering.

Andy staggered past him. When he got some distance away, he looked over his shoulder, but the man was still sitting on the crate, staring straight ahead, the twenty-dollar bill still lying on the sidewalk some two feet from the man's torn shoes.

When Andy arrived at his brother's place, desperate to crawl onto the inflatable mattress, bury his head in the blankets, and just fall asleep, he knocked at the door a few times, but there was no answer.

"It's me. Andy," he said. He hoped Candice would answer. He did not want to face Taylor at the moment, though Candice would likely be unenthusiastic too.

When there was no answer, he jiggled the knob a few times—the door was, unsurprisingly, locked. He took out his phone and called Taylor, but the call rang and rang with no answer.

He left a voicemail.

"Hey . . . it's Andy. I'm sorry it's late. Can you let me in?"

He waited a minute, but there was no call or text back.

He leaned against the door, listening for the sound of anyone, but it was quiet.

He banged on the door a couple times. "Come on, man. It's Andy. Let me in."

But the door remained unanswered.

He called Candice, but she didn't answer either.

After another couple minutes, where Andy continued jiggling the knob and pushing his shoulder against the door, hoping he could make it budge, he lay down in the hall, hugging himself against the frosty air conditioning that was blasting for some reason. His clothes were wrinkled and wet, his suit coat was gone, his eye was swollen. The hall light was on, glaring a little too brightly, but Andy couldn't see a switch anywhere.

He shivered in the fetal position, clutching his eyes shut and hoping to lull himself to sleep, but all he could think about was that homeless man on the corner, who had it much, much worse, and in a way, the more he thought about it, no matter how hard he tried not to, the whole weekend felt like mostly Andy's fault.

19

Andy awoke to Taylor standing over him, Taylor's eyes looking bloodshot, his normally clean-shaven face flecked with stubble.

The hall light was still on.

The air conditioning was still pumping.

Taylor stared at his brother another moment, Andy opening his eyes all the way, save for his right eye, which was still slightly shut because of the slap, before Taylor turned around and walked back into the apartment, leaving the front door open.

When Andy got to his feet, his body hurting all over, he walked inside the apartment, slightly limping. His brother was sitting on the couch, the TV on mute, the apartment quiet.

The wall clock said 7:05 a.m.

"Where's Candice?" Andy finally said.

"She left," Taylor said, stone-faced, as he stared at the muted TV.

Andy glanced at the screen, seeing a guy with glasses holding a cantaloupe and a kitchen knife. In the bottom right corner of the screen it said, *Kitchen Klutz.*

"*Left* left?" Andy asked.

"Yep."

"Oh." Andy put his hands in his pockets and then pulled them back out. "I'm sorry."

"Are you really?" Taylor's voice rose in volume. "Cause I don't think you are."

Andy lowered himself to the chair in the corner, his body relaxing a bit.

"I'm just not gonna answer that," Andy finally said. He *did* feel bad for his brother, but it was hard not to see Candice as the right one.

"And what happened to you? Jeez."

Andy let out a single laugh. "I had a rough night, you could say."

"I think we both did."

"Yeah."

And for the moment, Andy recognized he and his brother had something in common.

He turned to the TV where the cooking show host was juggling pears.

"This is the dumbest show," Andy said after a moment, hoping to perhaps lighten the mood, but then he looked toward Taylor and saw his face had fallen into a crumple, Taylor choking back tears.

"I'm fucked," Taylor said in a pinched voice.

Andy stared at his brother, but the glee he normally would've felt at Taylor finally having some sort of self-awareness wasn't inside of him.

He staggered to his feet and moved to the couch, where he sat next to Taylor, and pulled him into a hug, Taylor not pushing him away but instead burying his head in Andy's shoulder, the whole thing feeling bizarre at first, but he held his crying brother anyway, Andy feeling pathetic and lost but that Taylor was probably feeling the same way too.

Perhaps they were twins after all.

20

A ndy sat on the L with his suitcase by his feet and his backpack on his lap, the train crowded, as he headed toward Union Station, so he could get on Amtrak and return to Kansas City.

He spotted a girl, not too far from his age, a large purse over her shoulder, standing, holding onto the pole, her body swaying as the train bounded down the tracks. Then he noticed she was pregnant, her stomach looking burdensome on her slight frame.

Andy jumped to his feet, taking out his ear buds.

"Excuse me?" he said. She turned to him. "Please." He motioned to his now empty chair.

"Oh, thank you. That's so sweet." She moved to Andy's seat, gently lowering herself down. "Thanks."

An elderly woman in the row in front of her turned and smiled. "How much longer do you have?"

"Just another six weeks."

"Ah," the elderly woman said, looking nostalgic. "I had six of my own. Six. Can you believe it?"

"This is just my first," the girl said, laughing, still panting. "It's been so hard, but I can't wait to meet him." She placed her hand on her stomach, rubbing her striped shirt.

The elderly woman chuckled. "It's only going to get harder, but you can do it. You can. We all find a way to get through it, and it's the best thing you'll ever do. Trust me." The woman smiled warmly. "You at least have a little help?—oh sorry, I don't mean to be intrusive."

"Yes. My husband. I don't think he knows just how much work it's going to be, ha, but he's gonna be a good father."

"Good. Good," the woman smiled and turned to the front.

Andy watched, taking it all in, thinking about what it meant, and what it meant for him, and he couldn't shake the feeling that maybe he had really messed up.

After he got off the L, he began the quarter-of-a-mile walk to Union Station, ready to start moving past the last few days, but his legs were shaky, and his mind was racing.

Really . . . maybe it *could* work. It would be tricky, unusual, but people had done it. People had made it work.

He had felt a connection that had been eluding him for a long time.

And when he got to the front of Union Station, he just couldn't shake it anymore.

He pulled out his phone, his heart pounding—pushing, pushing—and when she answered, his voice almost cracked with relief.

"Hey!" Andy said. "So listen, I'm sorry about last night. I just . . . freaked out."

"It's okay," she said, her voice sounding small. "It's a big thing. I understand."

"Listen, where are you? I'm supposed to leave in a couple hours, but I want to see you. We can figure something out. I don't know what, but I want to."

People buzzed by Andy on the sidewalk. Nearby a young girl stopped to tie her shoe.

"Oh. Well, I'm in San Francisco."

"What? How—"

"We just landed. I left early this morning."

"Oh. Well . . . okay. But okay, I thought about it some more, and I just really like you. Sorry this isn't coming out more articulate—I didn't plan this. I just had to call and say something. So . . . I think we should figure something out. I recognize the baby thing is a big thing, and geographically it's a tricky situation, but plenty of people do that, and why not us? I normally avoid planes at all costs, but maybe in a couple weeks I could fly out and visit, and we could—"

"Andy." Her voice trailed off. She inhaled. "I'm on my way to my boyfriend's."

The phone fell silent.

The glaring absence of "ex" before "boyfriend."

More people hurried by Andy. The sun peaked over tops of buildings.

"We talked this morning," Shannon said. "We decided we're going to give it another try. We're going to at least try to work things out. He admitted he got scared and freaked out."

"And you're okay with him freaking out?" Andy said, his voice raising.

"You did too."

"Ah. Yeah."

"I know it's a messed-up situation. Maybe I'm stupid, but he's the father of my child. He was my boyfriend of seven years. I still love him. He says he still loves me."

The air inside Andy spilled out slowly like a leak from a gym ball.

"Yeah . . . no, that's . . . yeah . . . I guess that's probably for the best."

"You're a great guy, but you're also someone I knew for just three days."

"No, yeah, it's . . . I understand." Andy nodded slowly even though she wasn't standing in front of him. "Well, best of luck to you, Shannon. I really mean that. I think you'll be a good mom."

"Thanks. Best of luck to you too."

21

At 3:00, Andy boarded the train and found his assigned seat, an aisle seat next to a thin, late-fifties woman with long stringy hair and an iPad in her lap.

"Hi, I think I'm right here."

"Sure. Hi," she said, before turning her attention back to the iPad, which had a game of solitaire on it.

Andy sat back, settling into the chair and looking around the train. If he could, he hoped to sleep this entire ride back.

But then his eyes were drawn to a man a few rows ahead.

"I'll be right back," he said to the woman who didn't respond.

He walked a few feet and tapped Jerry on the shoulder.

"Uh-huh?" Jerry said, turning and looking up, before recognition came over his face. "Andy!"

"Jerry. Hi."

They shook hands, a smile coming over Jerry's face.

"What a nice surprise!" Jerry said.

"Taking the train back west?"

"Yeah. She's beautiful this time of year."

"Cool. Well, I'm sitting a few rows back." With his thumb he pointed over his shoulder. "I'm going to try to get some sleep, but . . . well . . . if you feel like chatting in the observation car later, I could be up for that."

"Oh yeah? Great! I'd like that."

"Cool. Well, see you later, then."

"See you later, Andy."

Andy returned to his seat, his body tired and still aching. The train soon began chugging forward, and then the announcements were made over the intercom, and the conductors walked through the train car, checking tickets. And later, when they were passing through Joliet, around forty-five miles or so out of Chicago, Andy caught a glimpse of Jerry, sitting in his seat, arms folded, sound asleep, and Andy had the feeling that things continue to move forward, and he was moving too, and he would continue to move. He would continue trying to keep up.